Candlelit Calamity

Copyright © 2024 by London Lovett

All rights reserved.

No part of this book may be reproduced in any form or by any electronic or mechanical means, including information storage and retrieval systems, without written permission from the author, except for the use of brief quotations in a book review.

ISBN: 9798879113884

Imprint: Independently published

CANDLELIT CALAMITY

FROSTFALL ISLAND
COZY MYSTERY SERIES

LONDON LOVETT

MAINLAND
OLD MAN
OF THE NORTH
SWIMMING BEACH
ISLAND DRIVE
CALICO PEAK
NORTH
POND
TEA, TARTS &
TITTLE-TATTLE
TEA
N
W
E
S
ICE CREAM
STAND
MOON RIVER
BURT'S BICYCLE
RENTAL
FISH & CHIPS
BIKES
CALICO TRAIL
BAYBERRY
HARBOR
OLIVE EVERHEART'S
COTTAGE
SALTY BOTTOM
FERRY
FROSTFALL HOTEL
CHICORY TRAIL
PRODUCE
STAND
MOON RIVER
BOARDING HOUSE
1000 STEPS
BEACH
SOUTHERN LADY
NATURAL AREA
PIRATE'S GOLD
RESTAURANT
FINNEGAN'S
POND
BEACH PLUM TRAIL
FROSTFALL HISTORICAL SOCIETY
& MARITIME MUSEUM
SOUTHERN LADY
LIGHTHOUSE
FROSTFALL ISLAND

one

A GUST of wind chilled my face. I closed my eyes until it settled back down to a breeze. Huck pushed his nose against my leg. He felt it, too. The dog was more intuitive than most when it came to the weather on Frostfall Island, our home for nearly ten years.

My gloved hand patted the top of his head. "Yep, Huck, I agree." The island was constantly being tickled, ruffled and even, on occasion, pummeled by the coastal winds, but the unexpected burst of energy carried with it the promise of a storm. How severe it would be was hard to predict, but my own intuition told me we were about to get a dose of winter that we wouldn't soon forget.

It was still early as Huck and I hiked along Chicory Trail. On these long, shadowy mornings I didn't bother with my watercolors unless there was something noteworthy in the landscape to capture. But a brittle January, made even less enjoyable by relentless glacial temperatures, had stripped the trees and shrubs of any signs of life. My normally lush, colorful, wonderful home looked like it was part of an apocalyptic movie set. I was thankful for the always stalwart evergreens, the white pines and the blue spruce trees that dotted the island and lined the path up to Calico Peak. They were a reminder that the earth was still alive and energetic and waiting for its return to glory beneath the bristly and naked trees and shrubs.

The sun had barely winked in the eastern sky. It promised to be a clear morning and, possibly, day, but standing at the tip of the trail, where the island ended in steep cliffs and a long stretch of sand known as Thousand Steps Beach, I could see a band of dark clouds that looked anything but friendly. It was too early to tell if the clouds were heading toward the island. Sometimes a storm at sea missed us entirely on its way to drop icy rain on the mainland. Occasionally, only the tail end slipped over us, giving us a nice, cold soaking and nothing more. And then there were those unlucky times when a ferocious storm plowed directly over us. On the mainland there were cities, buildings, storm drains and emergency services in place to help people weather a bad storm. On Frostfall, we were very much on our own. The residents of Frostfall loved the independence island living gave us, but in times of great calamities, like a brutal winter storm, that same independence could be daunting.

Huck's nose shot toward Olive Everheart's cottage and, most particularly, at her tray of peanuts. She left them out for the squirrels and birds in winter when the plants were no longer providing sufficient food. A squirrel sat hunched forward with a peanut in his paws. His tail was pulled up over his back, acting as a big fluffy shield from the cold. My dear friend Olive, an artist and longtime Frostfall resident, lived with her very vocal, musical parrot. She rarely left her cottage, so I visited her often with food and supplies.

I patted Huck on the head. "We need to get back to start breakfast, buddy."

The dog was reluctant to pull his attention away from the squirrel, but he followed and eventually trotted ahead of me. For many years, Huck and I hiked the same path, and we always stopped at the last wide curve on the trail to stare out at the ocean. It was the last place Huck and I stood to watch my late husband, Michael, motor out to sea on his fishing boat. One day he sailed off, and we never saw him again. It was terribly hard on me for years, and some recent events had caused me more grief. Not the same sadness and heartbreak I'd felt after his disappearance, but a new layer of grief mixed with confusion and even a few horrifying thoughts. Michael had been a seasoned fisherman. His boat, *Wild Rose*, was found months later, but Michael was gone and everyone assumed he'd fallen overboard. He was always stubborn about going out alone. He could never find the right help, and he was happier fishing on his own. After the boat was found, I never wanted to see it again, so I sold it at auction. The new owner recently came to the island to see me and to return a photo he was sure I'd been missing. Only the photo had nothing to do with me. A woman's arms were holding not one, but two babies, twins, and on the back was a handwritten note—"*Mikey, we need to talk.*" I'd never heard anyone call my husband Mikey. The photo was brutally perplexing. My mother had visited (an event in itself) and brought along photo albums. Tucked between the pages and pages of my sister Cora's two high-priced, lavish weddings were a few photos of Michael's and my simple ceremony. I noticed a strange woman in one of the reception photos. I had no idea who she was, and our guest list was small enough that it was easy to conclude she had not been invited. A little research into Michael's past, namely his high school yearbook, helped me put a name to the photo. Her name was Denise Fengarten. Michael dated her in high school. The few times we talked about our dating pasts, he mentioned that Denise was too clingy, and he broke it off. The yearbook provided me with another important and equally breath-stealing detail. Denise had handwritten in Michael's yearbook, calling him Mikey, and the handwriting matched the writing on the photo. I had no idea why Michael was keeping a photo of Denise's twins in his wheelhouse, but none of the explanations I came up with were good. The whole thing had left me feeling as if I'd fallen in love with and married a complete stranger.

Fortunately, now I was surrounded by my quirky Moon River Boarding House family, including my extravagant and impractical-in-all-aspects sister and the man who had quite recently stolen my heart. For the first month or so after Nathaniel joined our household, I wasn't entirely sure he'd fit in with the rest of the bunch. He was dealing with his own setbacks in life and came to the island to escape all of it. He'd been a detective on the mainland, and after years of trying unsuccessfully to track down a serial killer, the infamous Pillow Talk Killer, he'd left behind his badge and gun and found solace and a new job on the island. This job came with a hammer and work boots and, so far, had been satisfying enough to keep Nate on the island. I hoped I had something to do with that, too.

With the boarding house in sight, Huck raced ahead. His tail started spinning like the blades of a helicopter, which told me Nate was heading our way. Huck adored him and only pulled out the helicopter tail for his friend.

I couldn't hold back a laugh when I spotted Nate. He had on so many layers, he could barely walk.

"I assume you've seen the movie 'A Christmas Story,'" I said between laughs.

Nate held his arms straight out. His lunch cooler dangled from his right hand. His thermos was tucked into the pack on his back. I'd filled it with a pot of hot coffee. "Do I look like Randy in his snowsuit? That's the effect I was going for. I've been working on the outside walls of the lighthouse. Standing on scaffolding three stories up with the relentless ocean breeze feels like I'm standing in the Arctic."

"I can't blame you for layering up. It's not an enviable job in this brutal weather." I threw my arms around him. I laughed again. "It's like hugging a polar bear. Not that I've ever hugged one, and if I did, I'd probably regret it, but it's what I imagine a polar bear would feel like in my arms."

Nate lowered his mouth to mine for a kiss. "That polar bear doesn't know what he's missing."

"I'm not sure this conversation could get any sillier," I

said. "On a more serious note, a little predawn wind this morning had whispers of an incoming storm. And the offshore clouds look angry."

"Whispers of an incoming storm. Angry clouds," Nate repeated. His navy-blue eyes matched the sky in the distance. "You would make the world's most adorable and poetic weatherperson. The boss said something about a possible storm. I guess we don't have clarification on which way it's headed, but he said we might be off for a few days. And I'm, of course, heartbroken knowing that instead of standing in a blustery wind on top of rickety scaffolding with numb fingers and a frozen nose, I'll be cuddled up on the sofa with my sweetie and some of her delicious baked goods."

"Well, if you're already dreaming up that scenario, then I better do some baking. I'm planning to prepare a lot of food in case we're all stuck in the house for a few days. I also need to take some food over to Olive today. I want to make sure she's ready for the storm."

Huck barked on the back step. "You better get twinkle paws back into the house before he gets frostbite," Nate said. He kissed me again. "See you later."

"Have a good day and stay warm. Or at least reasonably warm."

two

THE SUN WAS STARTING to light the day. Winston was the only person up and about. He had a blue beanie pulled down low over his mop of thick blond hair. He was also wearing a look of concern that I hadn't seen in a long time. Winston was the youngest member of the Moon River family. He worked at a wildlife rescue at the northern edge of the island. The rest of us were occasionally treated to the company of one of their many rescues. Whenever an animal was too young to be left alone or there were too many animals at the rescue, Winston brought one of them home. After spending a delightful week bottle feeding and snuggling a baby lamb that had been left motherless, we all decided to go vegetarian. Winston was more than pleased about it. I put a lot of my old recipes in storage, possibly forever, and started filling my recipe boxes with delicious meatless meals.

"Everything all right, Winston?" I asked as I filled the coffee pot.

"Everything will be fine as long as that storm slips past the island."

"Not looking too good," Tobias said as he came into the kitchen. Tobias, a financial advisor and accountant, was in his fifties, but he kept as trim as an athletic teenager by swimming in the harbor every morning. But this weather was too cold even for him. It was his second day without his morning swim. It usually made him grumpy, so I made sure to put extra coffee in the filter. "I just saw the weather report," Tobias continued. "Last night they were giving us a forty percent chance of a direct hit. This morning it's fifty-fifty. Never good odds." Tobias was a numbers man.

"Not bad odds either," I added after seeing despair grow on Winston's face. "Are there a lot of animals at the sanctuary right now?" When Winston first moved in, we would have nice, long chats at the breakfast table. He was almost always the first person up, so we had time to talk without the others interrupting. During our private chats, I learned that Winston had a huge crush on Alyssa, the woman who ran the wildlife rescue. That crush lingered unreciprocated for months until he discovered that Alyssa felt the same about him. Now we hardly saw him. I was sure I'd have a room for rent soon in the boarding house, but so far, Winston hadn't mentioned the "M" word. His generation was cautious about the whole legal paper commitment. After what I'd gone through in the past few months, with Michael's high school girlfriend and the photos, maybe there was something to their hesitancy.

"We're at about half full right now. But there are a few birds, a gull and a pelican, that are quite sick, and they need to be looked after night and day. The storm is only making their situation more precarious. I'm sure we'll have to bring them inside Alyssa's living quarters if it gets bad. This morning we're going to check pens and start putting up canvas and wood to protect the more exposed enclosures. We've got to check supplies and make sure the generators and flashlights are ready."

"You should always prepare for the worst," Tobias said. He had a stern brow this morning, and he said it like a scowling father. I quickly filled his cup and set it down in front of him. A few sips and the scowl would disappear.

"I've got my own checklist," I said. "I'll be preparing lots of food to get us through the next few days."

Winston shook his head. "If the island takes a direct hit, you won't see me until it passes. I need to stay and help Alyssa."

"Of course," I said. "I could make extra if you want to stop by the house and pick it up."

"That's kind of you, Anna. That would be great. I'll come back to the house after I finish securing the pens."

"Do you have times for eggs?" I asked. "I've got fresh biscuits keeping warm in the oven."

Winston grinned. "Already helped myself to a few with butter and jam. Hope that's all right."

"Certainly. Say hello to Alyssa for me," I said as Winston headed out the door.

Two sets of footsteps preceded what seemed to be a ridiculous debate about which creamer flavor was the best. Opal stepped into the kitchen first. She was an eccentric retired teacher who spent most of her day in floral-print housecoats watching classic movie marathons. That wasn't the eccentric part though. Opal also, in her heart of hearts, believed that in a previous life she strolled around early 20th century Hollywood as none other than Rudolph Valentino. We'd all come to accept it as fact, even though we had no proof. Opal was smart and intuitive and a great housemate, so who were we to question it? And as eccentric as dear Opal was, she was mundane compared to my sister, Cora. My sister, in all her vibrant, forty-plus beauty, floated in behind Opal. She was wearing a dark green silk blouse over black leather slacks, a highly impractical outfit for a wintry day on the island, but for Cora, it was sensible. Her expensive, designer wardrobe pieces were the only souvenirs from two marriages to billionaires, both of which ended with the extremely aged groom dying shortly after the nuptials. Cora was still clinging to the coffee creamer debate.

"The eggnog one tasted nothing like eggnog. Besides that, a good eggnog is laced with expensive brandy, so the artificial creamer is way off the mark," Cora didn't follow politics or current events, but she was putting in her two cents about the creamer as if it was world news.

Both women loved to have the last word, so I waited for

Opal's reply before interrupting the crucial discussion with the scrambled or soft-boiled question.

"I still think your beloved pumpkin spice creamer is lacking all the qualities required for the coveted pumpkin spice label." Opal poured herself a cup of coffee. Their entire debate was a waste of energy. I no longer had any of the special holiday creamers on the coffee tray. We were back to non-dairy and real cream.

Cora had no good comeback for Opal's comment, so she shrugged as if none of it mattered (which, technically, it didn't) and sat down with a huff. "I can't believe Sera is keeping the teahouse open when we are so clearly in the path of a terrible storm."

After many years of being taken care of by rich boyfriends and husbands, Cora was finally earning her own wages at my best friend, Seraphina Butterpond's, teahouse. I'd coaxed Sera into hiring Cora. For the first few weeks I worried that the whole idea would end in disaster. Instead, my sister stepped right into the role of tea server, and, as was always the case with my sister, she charmed everyone who came in for tea.

"The weather channel says we have a fifty percent chance of a direct hit," Tobias said as he covered his eggs in salt. Showering his food with salt was one of his more notable habits.

"Maybe we'll get lucky, and it'll miss us altogether," I said. "And you can't expect Sera to shut down her business on the threat of a storm. I'm sure she'll close up if things start to look more menacing. By the way, I'll walk with you this morning. I need to get some produce for soups and chili. I'm going to make some food in case we're stuck home for a few days."

"See," Cora said. "You admit that we're about to get blasted by the storm."

"No, but I want to be ready in case it happens. If it doesn't, then I'll be ahead on meal prep, which means I'll have spare time to enjoy the weekend. Now, soft-boiled or scrambled?"

"Scrambled," Opal said with confidence at the same time that Cora said soft-boiled.

They looked at each other as if a new topic had come up for debate.

"Nope, one debate a morning, please," I said.

Tobias chuckled into his fork of food. I knew the coffee would wash away the grumps.

I leaned into the oven and pulled out the tray of biscuits that had been warming inside. "You know, I think I'll make some cinnamon rolls for Sunday morning breakfast. Should I make them with or without a glaze?" I asked. I was about to get two different answers from the women at the table. I put up my hand. "Never mind. I'll decide later."

three

CORA STOPPED HALFWAY along the trail to flick some drops of moisture off the fur trim on her boots. My sister had learned the hard way, with at least two painful falls on her bottom, that she had to skip her impractical high heels when walking to work. She'd saved up all her summer tips to buy herself an overpriced, extravagant pair of faux fur-lined snow boots for the trek to Sera's. She also learned quickly that fur lining might look lush and pretty, but it made your feet sweat (sweaty feet were neither lush nor pretty). She easily solved the problem by carrying her spiky, expensive designer shoes in her bag and changing once she got to work. Sera and I marveled at how easily she moved around delivering trays of hot tea and tarts on treacherous heels, all without spilling a drop.

The sky over the harbor was still blue, but the wharf and marina seemed eerily quiet. Even the gulls were subdued. There was no storm yet, but it seemed everyone was holding their breath waiting for it to crash into our humble little island. "I wonder who decided fur lining and trim in winter boots was a good idea," I said as we continued our trek.

"Gucci, that's who," Cora said flippantly to let me know my sarcasm would not deter her from wearing them.

We both stopped when a cold, withering wind stuttered through the landscape. Bare shrubs and trees seemed to duck down to avoid it. Cora shivered and zipped her coat higher so that it was right under her chin. "What kind of harsh, faraway planet have you brought me to, Anna?"

I laughed. We both hunkered down to avoid the cold snap carried through by the wind. "I didn't bring you here at all. You arrived, desperate for a place to live because the death of your second husband left you with a lot of beautiful, impractical clothes and jewelry and nothing else."

"Yes, but why couldn't you have had a boarding house on Maui or in Beverly Hills?"

"I'm sorry. You're right. Next time, I get the idea to start a boarding house, I'll check the Beverly Hills real estate listings."

Cora huffed. She was the one person I knew who could make an exasperated huff look elegant. "It's always about sarcasm with you."

"That's 'cuz you make it so darn easy," I said.

Cora lifted her chin and picked up her pace. Her fancy boots kicked up little puffs of white as she stomped along the trail.

I hurried to catch up to her, which wasn't difficult considering her fashionable boots were stiff and unwieldy. "I'll make it up to you by baking your favorite ginger-molasses cookies today."

Her chin was still lifted. "If it makes you feel better."

I was holding back a grin as we walked into the tea shop. Sera's shop, Tea, Tarts and Tittle-tattle, was an island favorite. People came across from the mainland just to have some of her delicious tarts and exotic teas. The locals came mostly for the tittle-tattle. It was a great place to hear gossip and find out what was happening in everyone's lives on the island. But in the middle of winter, gossip was slow and so was Sera's business. Fortunately, busy spring and summer seasons made up for it.

Cora hurried to the back to put on her apron and change her shoes to an even more impractical pair. Sera must have caught me smiling on the way in. I sat on my favorite stool. She was already pouring me a cup of my favorite oolong tea. It had a woodsy scent but was also a little spicy. It was a great tea for a cold morning.

"Looks like you two had a nice, sisterly chat on the way in. Cora swept through like an elegant but angry swan, and you entered like the cat who swallowed the canary."

"So, my sister is an elegant swan, and I'm a greedy, bird-eating cat?"

"I did say angry, too." Sera forced a smile. "I saved you one of my buttery pecan tarts."

"Nice save, my friend."

The shop had only a few regulars this morning, but the rest of the tables were empty. Sera's amazing husband, Samuel, came out from the stockroom. "Hey, Anna, so what do you think?" He gazed out the window. "Are we going to get hit or not? Sera just ordered me to drag all the outdoor tables to the storeroom."

Sera came out with a whipped cream-topped pecan tart. "I hardly think you could classify it as an order. You make me sound like a drill sergeant." She placed the tart down in front of me.

Samuel stood up extra straight and pushed out his big chest. "Samuel, you need to bring that furniture in right now or it'll get ruined by the storm." He relaxed and looked at me for my opinion. I'd learned many things in my forty-plus years and not stepping into a marriage squabble was one of them. I picked up the tart, smiled at both of them and took a bite.

"Good save, my friend," Sera quipped.

The door opened and a rush of cold air was followed by four women, not locals. They were dressed in stylish winter gear. They were unzipping coats and pulling off hats and gloves as they walked to a table in the back. One of the women, an attractive brunette, seemed to be arguing with a platinum blonde who had a curtain of bangs over her blue eyes. "I can't possibly sleep on that top bunk. I have to get up several times in the night to go to the bathroom. I'll forget and fall right onto the floor."

The blonde rolled her eyes. "You won't forget. You're just making up excuses. We drew numbers, and you got the top bunk. It's only fair."

They were forty-plus and, from the looks of it, successful women, but they were arguing like kids. Another woman with dark hair, glasses and a sallow complexion spoke up to end the argument.

"Look, Rachel, I'll take the top bunk, and you can have the single bedroom. I don't mind. I used to sleep in a top bunk at my grandmother's farm, so I look forward to sleeping up there. It'll bring back all those nice memories."

Rachel looked mildly contrite. "Are you sure, Toni? That's so sweet of you," Rachel said before Toni could take back the offer. "Thanks."

The fourth woman was wearing her red hair in braids. She looked sporty and fit. "Just like in high school—good ole Toni stepping in to keep the peace."

They all laughed at her remark—Toni the least.

Cora finally stepped out from the back. The fluffy boots were gone, replaced by bright blue heels. "We might be closing up early," Sera told her. "Depends on the weather." She walked past Cora to carry the list of teas to the women's table.

Cora sighed loudly. "Why couldn't she have just closed for the day?" she said in a whisper. "I could be in bed or taking a hot bath." She circled around to start filling tea kettles. Sera stayed at the table and talked to the women for a few minutes. She returned and handed Cora their orders. Sera leaned over the counter to talk in a lower voice.

"They're here for an annual meetup. They all went to high school together," she said.

I nodded. "That's what I gathered as they were arguing about the bunk bed. Too bad they picked this weekend to travel to the island."

"That's what I told them, but they've been on a waiting list to get into the Meyer's rental. It's the top-rated Frostfall rental on all the vacation sites."

"It's a nice place but not sure if it's worth staying here during a storm," I said.

"They said they didn't mind a little rough weather because they're from Vermont. I don't think they realize just how bad a storm could get out here on the Atlantic. Still, they'll be comfortable enough in the Meyer house. Jane had the kitchen remodeled this summer, and it's gorgeous."

"That's right. Your house is right next door." I sipped the last of my tea. I needed to get to the produce stand. Molly might be planning to close early too.

"Yeah, it's kind of annoying always having short-term renters next door, but Jane and Harvey keep the place looking nice, and they're picky about who gets to rent it. I'm sure those four will drink wine, talk and gossip, catch up on old times, and we won't hear a peep out of them."

"I'm sure that will be the case." I stood up. "I need to go buy produce for soup and chili and oranges for an orange bundt cake. I'm going to fill the larder, as they say, just in case that grumpy old storm decides to head our way."

Cora swept by with her tray of tea and not a word.

"Speaking of grumpy," Sera noted.

"She wants to be home in a hot bath," I said.

"Who doesn't?" Sera laughed. "Well, if the storm hits, I guess we'll see you on the flip side."

four

MOLLY PICKERING, my good friend and the woman who ran the local produce stand, was dressed head to toe in lime green snow gear. She was standing next to another dear friend, Frannie Bueller, the woman who ran the Frostfall Island Ferry. Frannie had one of her signature handknitted scarfs piled around her neck and the bottom half of her face. Both women were staring at their phones with looks of concern. I was sure I knew why.

"Don't tell me—we're going to take a direct hit," I said as I reached the rows of baskets.

Frannie looked up first. "We're at a seventy percent chance now. Not exactly promising odds."

"That's still a thirty percent chance that it won't happen," Molly said brightly.

"Remind me never to take you to Vegas." Frannie pushed her phone into her pocket. "The harbor is already getting choppy. I'll probably only risk one more crossing before parking *Salty Bottom* in the slip and heading home."

Frannie's expression grew grim. She knew that the harbor would be too dangerous to cross, which meant we'd be cut off from the mainland. Even helicopters wouldn't dare trying to get to the island.

Both women looked far more worried than I liked to see. They were both longtime islanders, and they knew when a worrisome storm was headed our way.

"Look, guys, we don't know yet if it's going to hit here, and we don't know how severe it'll be if it does make landfall."

"They're predicting eighty mile per hour gusts and heavy sleet and snow," Frannie said. "The hotel is putting up sandbags to prepare for the storm surge."

"All right, well, if you're going to be all 'doom and gloom' about it," I said.

"Not doom and gloom. It's what I heard over the radio from the Coast Guard." Sometimes Frannie could be gruff. Today seemed to be her day for that, but I couldn't blame her. People would be expecting Fran and her husband, Joe, to do something about being stranded in the storm. They were both experienced captains and knew when the harbor was too dangerous to cross.

"Well, if it helps, I'm going to bake some goodies and make a giant vat of chili." I glanced at the baskets. Molly had some beautiful russet potatoes for sale. "And I think I'll buy these potatoes and makes some buttery, cheesy twice-baked potatoes. Everyone is welcome at Moon River. I'll make plenty."

"Yum, it's been a long time since I've had twice-baked potatoes," Molly said. I'd taken her mind off the storm for now, but Frannie still had her mouth pulled tight in worry. Nothing, not even cheesy potatoes, was going to free her mind of the storm. "My grandmother used to make a thick mushroom gravy to pour on twice-baked potatoes," Molly continued.

"Gravy on top of cheesy, buttery potatoes," I said. "I never met your grandmother, but I have huge admiration for a woman who came up with that decadent combo. I might even try it."

"Still can't believe those five women came to the island this weekend for their traveling-pants-sisterhood thing," Frannie said. "I tried to tell them it was going to get rough and that we'd be cut off from the mainland until things calmed down, but they went on about how they were from Vermont and they'd survived some of the worst weather Mother Nature had to offer. I rolled my eyes and told them these Atlantic storms weren't anything like their blizzards, but they laughed it off. I guess we'll see how they manage when the lights go out and all the power is off."

Molly turned to Frannie. "Boy, someone woke up with a half empty glass today."

I chuckled too but Frannie's mood and expression had me worried. She knew storms better than any of us.

"I saw the women just now in Sera's place. They were very

excited about their weekend. Wait, did you say there were five? I only saw four."

Frannie rolled her eyes up. "That's right. Four came in on the nine o'clock ferry and then a fifth woman traveled alone on the ten o'clock. I didn't ask her why she was heading to the island. She looked the same age and, I don't know, the same style as the other women, so I just assumed she was going to join them. Guess I assumed wrong. That means there are five visitors on the island who have no idea what they're in for. I'd better get back to the ferry. There'll be a handful of people making their escape from the island now that we're at seventy percent. Bunch of dandelions, those people who live here most of the year but as soon as the weather gets rough, off they go to their mainland homes." The end of Frannie's long scarf fell loose. She tossed it back around her neck and headed toward the docks.

Molly and I watched her waddle away, hampered by her heavy winter gear.

"Wow, I've never seen her like that," Molly said. "Makes me think I should close early and head home to hunker down. I hadn't even thought about losing power, which is silly because we lose it even in mild storms. Gosh, I hope my flashlight batteries are still good."

"If not, I have a big supply. Just let me know if you need some." I started picking out the nicest and biggest potatoes. Having the oven on all day would warm the kitchen and fill the house with great smells. It was hard to be frantic about an incoming storm if the kitchen was filled with baked goods. I decided to bake especially fragrant goodies like orange bundt cake and ginger cookies. "I'm going to make some extra of everything to take to Olive. I worry about her at times like this and then I'm always pleasantly surprised when she floats right through these storms as if they're nothing at all."

"Still, I'm sure she'll appreciate all the goodies."

I picked out four bright and sweet smelling oranges. "These will be perfect for the bundt cake. Naturally, I'll be pouring on a citrus glaze."

"Now you've got my mouth watering. I think I'll make some peanut butter cookies. They're the perfect dipping companion for milk." She glanced back toward the docks. We could see Frannie because of her brightly colored scarf. "Frannie doesn't worry often. When she does—it makes the hair stand up on the back of my neck." Molly turned to me. "Do you think we'll be all right?"

"Sure, we will. We're Frostfallians. And I just made that up, but I think it works." I paid for my produce. "Let me know if you need those batteries. I'm going to check mine, too. There's nothing worse than trying to change the batteries in a flashlight after the lights have already gone out." I hugged Molly because Frannie had left her shaken. "I've got a spare room if you feel more comfortable riding this thing out in the company of friends."

"Thanks, Anna. I'm sure I'll be fine. I've got a stack of books to read and with those peanut butter cookies added into the mix, it should be a nice few days off. Besides, who knows, it might end up being just a few sprinkles of snow and gusts of wind." We both looked east toward the horizon as she said it. Those same dark clouds looked thicker, deeper and even angrier than before. All we could do was laugh about her optimism.

"My offer stands," I said. "I'm going to go home and get these potatoes baking and my bundt cake batter mixing."

"Bye, Anna. At least we know there won't be any murders this weekend. Everyone will be locked in their houses looking frantically for their flashlight batteries."

I waved back at her and smiled. I was the unofficial-yet-somewhat-official murder detective on the island. I had no badge, no gun, no training and absolutely no idea how I landed the role, but Molly was right. It wasn't a prime weekend for a murder. I sighed. If I thought about it, I actually looked forward to a few cozy days at home.

five

OPAL KEPT me company for my baking and cooking marathon. I even got her involved with squeezing oranges and chopping carrots and onions. As I hoped, while a churlish sky formed outside the window, the kitchen was filled with warm, comforting aromas. The potatoes had been baked, scooped, and refilled with a cheese and butter-laden filling. I wrapped them and put them in the freezer. I would pull them out for their all-important second baking when we were ready to eat them. I'd been tempted to make a mushroom gravy like Molly mentioned, but decided with all the desserts and other rich food we might be tipping the decadence scale a little too much.

Opal was making a new pot of coffee while I finished glazing the orange bundt cake. A drip of the glaze landed on my thumb. I licked it off. "Oh, wow, we outdid ourselves with this bundt cake, Opal. Tobias is going love it."

Opal turned on the coffeepot. "I'm not sure how much

credit I can take for that cake. All I did was squeeze the oranges."

"And you did a spectacular job."

Opal walked to the silverware caddy on the table and pulled out a spoon. She dipped it into the bowl of glaze and tasted it. "Hmm, you're right. I did do a spectacular job with those oranges." We both laughed. "Do you want a cup of coffee?" she asked.

"Yes, yes, yes."

"I'll take that as a yes then." Opal chuckled as she took two cups down from the cupboard. The aroma of coffee mingled with the citrusy smell of the cake. She poured us each a cup. "Come take a load off, Anna. You've been at that stove all day."

I spun the cake around on its pedestal stand. "Perfect. We'll have some tonight. It's a nice, bright dessert after a bowl of chili with crackers."

I sat across from Opal, and we sipped in blissful silence for a few minutes.

"I think I taste tested too many of your treats. Those molasses-ginger cookies are sublime, by the way."

"Thanks. The fresh nutmeg makes a difference. But I'm with you. Far too much taste testing." I looked around at the kitchen. After the hours of cooking and baking, it was a chaotic mess. "I think I used every mixing bowl and spoon."

"I can help you clean up," Opal said with about as much enthusiasm as a kid saying they'd clean their room. She yawned dramatically. "But I think I need to take a quick nap first."

"Don't worry about it. I've got a system for tackling this kind of industrial-sized mess, and it only works with one person."

Opal tried to put on a frown.

I laughed. "I can see you're heartbroken about it."

Huck hopped to his feet from a dead sleep. He raced to the door with the helicopter blade tail spinning. "Uh oh, looks like the construction site shut down for the day. They must have gotten word that the storm is a sure thing."

I walked over to my desk and picked up my phone. There was a text from Nate. "We're shutting down. Looks like Frostfall is in the direct path of the storm. I'm heading home to help get the house ready."

Nate walked in the back door as I put down the phone. "Just read your message. I haven't had time to check my phone until now."

Nate smiled at the clutter in the kitchen. "I can see why. It smells like heaven in here."

Opal yawned again. "Well, all this cooking has worn me out. I'm going up for a nap. Let me know if the house is floating away in the storm." Opal left the kitchen.

Nate placed his lunch cooler on the floor next to the kitchen counter. "I can help. I just need to get out of my polar bear outfit."

"Wait. I need one more polar bear hug before he disappears for good."

We stood in the fragrant, steamy kitchen in a long embrace. Every day I felt closer and closer to the man. I could no longer deny that he'd stolen my heart, and it seemed he felt the same way. The prospect of a major heartbreak was always poking at my worrywart side. Nate had come to the island to get away from his life on the mainland, one that had left him fraught with disappointment, but sometimes, after he spoke to an old friend or went mountain biking on the mainland with Sera's husband, Samuel, Nate would come back with an adventurous twinkle in his eye, a twinkle that seemed to look past the shores of our small island. When we got word that the infamous Pillow Talk Killer had claimed another victim on the mainland, Nate was visibly shaken, and he sank into a dark mood. He blamed himself because he'd failed to catch the killer. I was sure he'd head back to his old job, his need to find the killer renewed. But he stayed. At least for now. I was sure my constant worry about losing him had to do with losing Michael a year after we got married. Now Michael and the memories we shared together had been tainted. Nate had been there to help me get through the rough patches.

Nate kissed me. "And now, I'll remove these layers before I pass out from heatstroke. It's just a touch warmer in this kitchen than out on the scaffolding." He reached up to wipe some beads of sweat off his forehead. "Standing so close to my hot girlfriend isn't helping matters either."

Nate headed upstairs, and I got to work on my kitchen. I'd certainly outdone myself today, but now we had a lot of good food to eat while we waited out the storm. If the power went out, which was practically guaranteed, I could heat the vat of chili in the hearth. We had a generator that could power up the stove and oven in a pinch. Our power grid was connected to the mainland, and they were generally good about getting power back on quickly in these winter storms, but our little island was always last on the priority list.

I had most of the mixing bowls washed and ready to dry when my handsome helper returned to the kitchen. He stopped at the coffeepot first.

"Do you need anything to eat?" I asked.

"Nope. The sandwich, macaroni salad and brownie you packed me were delicious. Ate every last bite and didn't even trade my sandwich for a frog or new baseball. And yes, I traded for both those things when I was a kid. The frog didn't go over too well with my mom. She drove me up to the local pond to let him go."

"It was that frog's lucky day when he met up with your mom," I said. I held out a dry dishtowel, and he got to work drying the bowls.

"I've got to say, the only topic of conversation out on the worksite was about the storm. We've had a few good ones since I arrived on this island. There was that crazy summer storm with lightning and wind, and the rain was pelting the windows like bullets. And then there was that storm that dumped three feet of snow on the island. Something tells me this one is going to make those look like a kiddie ride at the carnival."

"I hope you're wrong about that, but Frannie looked really worried this morning. That tells me we're in for a thrashing."

"What do you need me to do aside from drying dishes?" he asked.

"After we straighten up the kitchen, we can check the

flashlights to make sure they're working. I've got a box of candles, and I'll pull all my candleholders out and place them in safe spots around the house. We should check to make sure all the windows are securely shut. Remember when Cora left her bedroom window open during that terrible summer storm? Took me forever to dry the carpeting in her bedroom."

I glanced out the window. The sky seemed to be glowering down at the island. "You know what? I'm almost done here. Give me the towel and get started with the window check. We'll need more wood for the hearth. I might be heating food in it when the power goes off. Which reminds me, there's a gas can in the shed. The generator needs fuel."

A gust of wind pushed gently against the house. It was only a tiny sample of what we were going to experience. "Olive," I said on a gasp. "I've been so busy cooking, I forgot I planned to take her some food."

"I think we've still got a few hours before the storm reaches the island. I'll walk with you to Olive's. Let's get done with your checklist first." Nate walked toward the stairs to do the window check.

The first clap of thunder sounded in the distance. "Oh boy," I said quietly. "Here we go."

six

NATE and I had just finished with our storm checklist when Cora came home in her stylish, furry boots. "It's not a day to be out," she said as she started peeling off the layers. "The tea shop was empty, of course, so Sera had me doing inventory in the stockroom." Cora rolled her eyes. "You know what kept going through my head?" she asked.

"If only my snobby friends could see me now?" I asked. Nate chuckled quietly behind me.

"No. Besides, I didn't keep ties with anyone in those social circles. They're all a bunch of shallow bores, only interested in money," she said as she stepped out of her four-digit designer boots. "I thought, boy, wouldn't it be nice if my tyrannical boss let me leave early, so I could beat the monstrous storm home. Sera must have been reading my mind because she came into the stockroom and said—'it's getting pretty dark out there, why don't you head home.' It took me twenty seconds to change shoes and gear up."

"Then you raced out the door, leaving behind only the scent of your expensive French perfume and tufts of fur from your boots," I added.

"What? I better not have been shedding fur." She leaned down to make sure her boots were intact. "Before you hand me a list of chores to do so we can get ready for the storm, I'm going upstairs for a long, hot bath. And by long, I mean you might not see me until tomorrow morning."

Cora left the kitchen just as Tobias stepped in through the back door. "We are in for a doozy," Tobias said. He took off his hat and rain slicker. "I was locking up my office, and a wind slammed me from behind. It was only a short burst, but it sent a chill right through my bones." As he spoke, his eyes went right to the orange bundt cake. I'd cut a slice off to take to Olive's. Tobias looked at me. "I hoped I might get the first taste."

"Actually, you still can. That slice is wrapped up and destined for Olive's house."

Tobias's eyes rounded. "You're not going out there now, are you, Anna? This thing hasn't made landfall yet, but if these early winds and temperatures are any indication of what we can expect—"

"I'm walking with her, Toby," Nate said. "We won't be long, and I promise not to let a wind gust carry away our Anna."

"Good idea, Nate. I'm glad you're going along."

I laughed. "O.K. Ma and Pa, I've been living on this island long enough to know how to navigate a little cold wind."

Nate looked at me. "I'm Pa, right?"

Tobias laughed and I rolled my eyes.

"We should be on our way before we really do end up in trouble out there." A text came through as I put on my coat and hat. It was from Winston. "Staying here to help with the animals. Probably won't have time to stop by for goodies, but Alyssa is making soup and we're going to bake some cookies. You guys stay safe."

I wrote back. "You, too. See you soon." I put the phone in my pocket. "Winston is staying at the sanctuary, so it looks like our group is complete. Toby, we put a flashlight, candlesticks and matches in your room. I pulled out some extra blankets too in case we lose power. If it's out for a long time, then we can all huddle in front of the hearth in the front parlor."

Tobias nodded. "It sure is nice to have a place to stay warm and safe and well-fed," he added after eyeing the cake again.

"Help yourself to a slice, Toby. We'll be back soon." I handed Nate the basket to carry. I figured if he was tagging along to *keep me safe*, he might as well do the heavy lifting.

"Thank you, Anna." Tobias took off his coat and gloves. "And at the risk of being called Ma again—keep close to her." He winked at Nate.

"Sure thing, Ma." Nate patted the dog's head. "You stay here, Huck. I'm in charge of the little lady this time."

"Now you're just being annoying," I said.

We stepped outside as a wind gust swirled around the back of the house. I pulled my beanie down lower and adjusted my gloves so my fingers were snug inside. The dark mass of clouds that had been giving the island the evil eye since early this morning had moved much closer to shore.

I wrapped my arm around Nate's free arm and snuggled next to him. The trails that I traversed so often in the shadows of dawn, and even before those shadows took shape, looked far less inviting under the storm-darkened sky. The bare tree branches vibrated with each wind, making those normally innocuous branches look like angry claws. I giggled at the way my imagination worked.

Nate glanced over at me. "That's the way to keep things light. Just laugh in the face of danger."

"I wasn't laughing at danger. I was laughing at myself. It feels like we're walking through a haunted forest. It's strange but actual nightfall doesn't produce nearly as much darkness as those storm clouds."

Nate looked out at the ocean where the storm waited to make its grand entrance. "Those are some really black clouds. I wouldn't want to be out on a boat and find myself under that kind of sky."

"I agree. Let's pick up our pace." A streak of lightning temporarily lit up the clouds and the island. "We better not stay long either."

A few diligent squirrels were filling their cheeks with the last peanuts in the tray. "Ha, there's Charlie," Nate said.

I looked around. "Who's Charlie?"

"The squirrel. See that guy who is missing a chunk of fur from his tail? He and Huck have a longstanding feud going, so I thought I should name him. Charlie squeals and yells and raises his tiny fists whenever he sees Huck. I think Huck is afraid of Charlie, but don't tell him I told you."

"I'm out here almost every day with that dog, and I never noticed he had a problem with one squirrel in particular or that the squirrel was missing a chunk of hair." I looked over at him. "I guess that's why they paid you for your detective work, and I just get the occasional 'thank you' and 'good job.'"

Olive saw us coming up the path. She opened the door. "Not just one but two of my favorite visitors," she said as she waved us quickly inside. A fire was roaring in the hearth, and Johnny, the rock and roll singing macaw, started doing his dance across the back of the couch but didn't squawk his usual greeting. He was always shy when Nate was with me.

Olive took the basket from Nate. "Oh, Anna, you shouldn't have. I can't wait to unpack it." She smiled up at Nate. "It's like Christmas every time she brings the basket." She took a whiff of the food. "I smell so many goodies, I can't even make a guess. Definitely something with ginger."

"Molasses-ginger cookies. Nate is going to double check all your windows. Have you pulled out your flashlights?" Nate started his window check.

Olive had her long, wavy hair tied up in a bun on her head. She tapped her chin. "Now where did I put those flashlights?" She snapped her fingers. "They're under the kitchen sink." I nodded at Nate to check the batteries after the windows. Olive looked between both of us. "Do you think it's going to be a bad storm?"

"It looks like it. And the island is in its path." I helped her unpack the basket. "Why don't you and Johnny come to the boarding house for a few days? I've got a guestroom available, and there's tons of food."

Olive waved her arm over the basket. "I've got plenty here too." I knew she'd never go for the idea, but I always tried. "Johnny isn't comfortable anywhere but home. I'll be fine, Anna." She patted my hand. "It won't be my first big storm, and it won't be my last. Unless my time is up soon," she added, then laughed.

I hugged her. "If you're sure, but the offer stands. Nate and I will come get you no matter what's happening on the island."

"This old cottage knows how to stand up to those winds. I'll be fine. And I'd offer you both tea, but I don't want to keep you. These old bones are telling me that storm is knocking on the door this very minute."

Nate checked the windows and the flashlights. He carried in some more wood for the fire, then we hugged goodbye. "You two hurry," Olive said. "And thank you for the goodies. Can't think of a better way to sit out the storm than with your delicious baked goods."

We waved goodbye. Nate put his arm around my shoulders as we both hunkered down in our coats. As we passed the curve on Chicory Trail, the one with the vast view of the ocean, a great, bold streak of lightning lit up the sky and a clap of thunder followed that shook the entire island.

Nate dropped his arm from my shoulders and took hold of my hand. We all but ran back to the house.

seven

THE HOUSE RATTLED and vibrated and made sounds I hadn't heard before as a fierce wind thrashed the island, knocking out the power just before midnight. Heavy snow and chunks of hail the size of golf balls pelted the windows and turned the dreary, dark landscape into a treacherous, icy world. While we humans huddled in our blankets in front of a blazing hearth, snacking on ginger cookies and sipping cocoa, the island's more important inhabitants, the creatures that made the island unique and vibrant and wonderful, had to face the storm head on. I thought about little Charlie, Huck's squirrel nemesis, and the two geese that had made a permanent home on Finnegan's Pond. Something told me Winston and Alyssa would have their work cut out for them after this storm passed.

Once we determined that the power was not returning anytime soon, everyone reluctantly left their comfy beds and came downstairs to sit in the front parlor. It wasn't as if anyone was able to sleep with the clamor outside. Eventually, quilts and pillows were dragged down the stairs, too. Opal took the sofa. Tobias curled up on the right side of the hearth near the bookshelves, and Cora buried herself in her expensive downy quilt, one she'd bought herself as a birthday present, and curled up in a silky cocoon in the big reading chair. Nate and I slept directly in front of the hearth with a very frightened dog snuggled between us.

After a long night, things outside seemed to calm down a little. I was used to waking up before dawn. I scooted out from under the quilts. Huck grunted in his sleep. His paws were twitching and his nose kept wriggling. It was always comical to think about what a dog might be dreaming. Was Charlie in the dream? I patted Huck's head, and he settled back into a soft snore. Nate's dark lashes shaded his cheeks as he, too, snored softly. He was up most of the night keeping watch on the house and the fire and the storm in general. The power never returned, but the fire in the hearth had bathed the room in a warm glow. Once the wind and lightning had run out of energy, leaving us with only the occasional gust and lots of falling snow, everyone had finally dozed off. Something told me it would be a few hours before they woke, which was fine. It would give me time to get breakfast ready for when the power came back on. It didn't usually take too long once a storm slowed down.

I walked in sock-covered feet to the hearth. We'd all slept in multiple layers of clothes. I was wearing long underwear under sweats, but I could still feel the chill in the air. The fire had died down to red hot coals, mounds of ash and not much more. I added kindling and more wood to the dwindling fire. I moved as quietly as a mouse and as slowly as a sloth so as not to wake anyone, especially Nate. He'd only tucked himself in a few hours earlier. With any luck the fire would be roaring and warming the room by the time everyone peeled themselves out of their deep sleep.

I managed to get the fire going again without waking anyone. I walked softly toward the kitchen. The power popped back on. Appliances, clocks and the furnace made their loud clicking yawns. I froze in place and looked around the room. Everyone was fast asleep. Even Huck was still snoozing, and he rarely slept late.

I walked to the kitchen and picked up the coffeepot. There would be plenty of refills this morning. I stood at the sink, filling the pot as I looked out the window. Moon River was frozen over. Debris jutted out from the ice. Once it thawed, the river would turn on its self-cleaning mode, and the debris would be swept swiftly downstream. The backyard, the shrubs, the trails were all slick with ice. The occasional burst of wind blasted through, shaking some ice and snow free from the roof and trees.

I carried the pot to the coffee station I had set up on the sideboard. I was just about to add the coffee grounds when my phone rang from the front room. I'd turned the ringer all the way up because the storm was so loud. I'd kept the phone close by in case Molly or Olive or even Winston needed me. I raced back through to the front room. All my care not to wake anyone had been wasted. My loud, obnoxious ringtone had yanked everyone from a deep sleep. There were groggy, grumpy faces all around me as I reached the end table where I'd set my phone. I smiled sheepishly at everyone.

"Oops," I said and looked at the screen. "Sera. That's strange."

"I'm not working. Tell her the storm carried me away for good," Cora said sleepily. She lowered her head back beneath the quilt.

I walked away to answer it. It seemed everyone was willing to give sleep another try, and a phone conversation in the middle of the room was out of the question.

"Sera?"

"Thank goodness, Anna. I wasn't sure if you'd be awake. And I've been waiting for the darn power to come back on so I could call you."

"Is something wrong? Is Sam all right?"

"Yes, he's fine but severely shaken, and I can't get much out of him. He doesn't want to tell me the details." Sera was talking fast and not making much sense.

"Sera, I don't understand. Why is Samuel shaken? What details?"

Sera finally took a deep breath and slowed down. "Samuel and I were sleeping in front of the living room fireplace this morning when something woke both of us. At first, I thought it was an animal or some creature in distress, then it happened again. It was a scream, a woman's scream, and it was coming from next door, from Jane's house."

"Where the women are having their reunion?"

"Yes. Oh, Anna, the weather out there is terrible, but we need you. Something dreadful has happened in that house.

Naturally, when we realized it was a scream, Samuel got dressed, grabbed his baseball bat and went next door to see if there was an intruder or something. He found three of the women shivering and cold in front of the house, looking ghostly pale. One was even throwing up. They could barely talk or explain what was going on, but they pointed frantically inside and said something had happened to their friend, Rachel. He walked inside with his bat ready and then he found her." Sera's voice was shaky. "He came back white as a ghost and unable to speak for a few minutes. He wouldn't tell me what he saw, but he was sure the woman was dead. Then he said to call Anna."

The kitchen floor creaked. I spun around. Nate had walked into the room. His thick, long hair was a mess, and his five-o'clock shadow was dark and thick. He raked his hair back with his fingers and yawned before noticing the look on my face. He straightened from his drowsy slouch. "Is it Olive?" he asked.

I shook my head. "All right, Sera. Where are the women right now?"

"Samuel just went out to bring them over here. I'm heating up some coffee and tea."

"I'll be there as soon as I can." That comment made Nate stand up even straighter.

"Be careful, Anna. It's very slick out there. Samuel nearly fell on our front porch."

"I'll pull some spikes onto my snow boots and bring along ski poles. I'll see you soon."

Nate was ready with a million questions. "Why are you

going to Sera's? It's not safe out there. What could she possibly need you for?"

I held up my hand to stop the flow of questions. "A group of women came to the island for the weekend. They're staying in the house next to Sera's. Something awful has happened to one of them." I walked to the utility closet and pulled out my traction spikes and ski poles. I always used them on snowy hikes. "Sera and Sam woke to screams, and Samuel went to check on them. He won't give Sera many details, but he came back pale and in shock. He told Sera to call me, so I can only assume there's been a murder."

"I'm going with you," Nate said in a tone that left no room for argument. I was somewhat relieved. I didn't relish the idea of walking across a storm-ravaged, icy landscape on my own.

"I think Michael had a pair of microspikes for his boots." I dug through a few boxes and found the spikes.

"It'll only take me a few minutes to wash up and get dressed," Nate said.

"Me, too." I glanced out the window. I'd imagined staying inside in front of that fire, snacking and reading and napping all day. "I guess duty calls, and there's no rest for the weary and every other sentiment that fits this scenario. And Molly thought, if nothing else, the storm would stop any mayhem from happening on the island."

Nate and I walked toward the stairs.

"Mayhem does seem to follow you around, St. James," Nate said with a weak chuckle.

eight

"NOT AS BAD AS I EXPECTED." Nate's spiked boots crunched through piles of ice and slush. He leaned down, picked up a fallen tree branch and threw it into the landscape and away from the trail.

I glanced up at the sky above, only there was no sky, just dark clouds. You could almost see snarling faces laughing down at us. "I don't think we're out of the woods yet. We're just in a pocket of calm. Maybe the storm paused so we could get to our murder scene." I shook my head. "Maybe it's not a murder scene. I feel like I know Samuel well though, and he doesn't seem like the type of guy who would cause this kind of commotion unless something bad had happened."

"I agree. Sam and I have spent enough time together that I can say, without hesitation, that he's not someone who would be prone to panic or hysteria. He's about as calm a person as I've ever met."

"So true." I placed my foot in a spot that looked steady, but my ankle went sideways. Nate caught me by the elbow.

"You all right?" he asked.

"Yes, just a clumsy step. After talking about Samuel and his lack of panic, I'm sure we're about to face something horrifying." I looked out toward the harbor. "Help is a long and tumultuous boat ride away. No one in their right mind would attempt crossing that harbor unless they were on a tanker." The moored boats, including Frannie's quirky and slightly dilapidated *Salty Bottom*, were bobbing up and down on the choppy tide. The storm had churned up so much ocean floor the water was murky and brown. Even the gulls couldn't be bothered to fish in the sludgy mess. They'd found shelter under the eaves of the bike shop.

A brisk wind kicked up suddenly. Nate and I ducked to avoid being pelted by the cold drops of moisture it contained. Most of it was ice and snow coming off the trees. We waited for it to pass and then continued along the trail. Sera's house was still a mile away.

"I guess Mother Nature isn't through with us yet," Nate said. He picked up another branch and heaved it into the brush.

"Not in the slightest." Even with spiked boots and ski poles each step had to be carefully planned out to avoid a fall. It made the trek to Sera's painstakingly slow. "If the weather was nice, I would already be there." I started taking bolder, faster steps. Nate decided to leave the trail clearing for later and picked up his pace too.

"You mentioned these women came to the island for the weekend?" he asked as he caught up to my new pace.

"Yes, they came into the tea shop yesterday morning. Four of them, in their early forties and apparently all friends from high school. It was a reunion. Sera spoke to them and warned them a storm was coming. They laughed it off. They told Sera they were from Vermont and didn't mind a storm. They'd been on a waiting list to rent the Meyer house. It's that nice gray Cape Cod next to Sera's. It was rather comical because two of the women were arguing about who would be stuck sleeping in the top bunk in the double room. The debate finally ended when the woman who'd won the single room traded with the woman who was stuck on the top bunk." I stopped for a second. "Her name was Rachel. The woman who was complaining about being in the top bunk was named Rachel. That was the name of the dead woman. Maybe she should have stayed in that top bunk after all."

I was relieved when Sera's cute, butter-yellow house came into view. The Meyer house sat next to Sera's. It had gray shingles and white framed windows. The stone walkway up to the peach-colored front door was covered with icy footprints going both directions. It was easy to conclude most of the prints were made this morning when Samuel went to the house to help the women. It also meant that finding footprints that didn't belong, footprints that belonged to the killer, would be impossible on the front path.

Sera saw us coming up the road. She stepped out onto her front yard in just her sweats and instantly crossed her arms against the cold. "I'm so glad you're both here," she said as we reached her. "Now, I don't want to start any rumors, but they're talking about the Pillow Talk Killer in there."

I hadn't meant to turn my face Nate's direction so abruptly, but as soon as I heard mention of the serial killer, my reflexes pulled me that way. His jaw tightened some, but he had no comment. If it was true and the PTK had somehow found his way to the island, I was sure it would devastate Nate. He came to the island to find peace and solace. If the killer followed him here, then all the progress he'd made since coming to the island would have been erased.

Nate turned away from Sera and headed toward the neighboring house. I shrugged at Sera, and she offered me an apologetic smile. I followed behind. Walking on spiky shoes was never easy or graceful, and moving quickly across the frozen yards reminded me of that. Twice my boots got caught in slushy mud. I yanked my foot free and finally caught up to Nate at the front door.

He was layered in winter gear, but I could see how tense he was by his posture. He pushed open the front door and glanced at me. "I'm going in first," he said sharply.

I started to argue, but he shook his head. "I'm going in first," he repeated.

He pulled the microspikes off his shoes and disappeared into the house. I watched through the front door as he pushed open doors and swept the rooms with his gaze. The last door made him pause. He'd found the room with the victim.

"I'm coming in," I said as I took off my spikes and rested my ski poles on the porch.

This time Nate nodded without an argument. The heater was running at full speed, but the air from the open front door made the house cold. I smelled the metallic odor of blood as I walked down the short hallway. The house had been decorated to perfection with whimsical nautical decorations and sumptuous drapes and bedding.

Nate stepped into the room as I reached the doorway. I closed my eyes for a second to gather myself. I released the breath I'd been holding as I followed him. Rachel's gray, dead face peered halfway out of a pillowcase. Someone had pushed it up off her head. The blood on the bedding had spread down the side of the mattress and even dripped onto the floor. The words *Kiss, Kiss* were written in dark pink lipstick on the side wall. The one window in the bedroom sat open about six inches, and icy air seeped through.

Nate was at Rachel's bedside. He leaned down to get a closer look at the wound in her chest. "Looks like she was stabbed." His voice was calmer than I expected. In fact, the earlier tension was gone, and his shoulders were more relaxed. Even his jaw had loosened up. I worried he was in shock and that this whole thing would hit him like a ton of bricks.

I walked closer to the bed. It was an awful scene, and it was easy to understand Samuel's reaction. "Is it—" I didn't know how to form the question and wasn't entirely sure I should ask it. But I needed to know. Everyone on the island needed to know. Everything in front of me seemed to point to the PTK, the pillowcase, the victim stabbed in bed, the lipstick message. "Nate," my throat was dry, "was it the PTK?"

There was a long pause before he answered. "No. This was a copycat murder. I've seen a few in the past years. That's why we keep some details out of the press."

It felt disrespectful to poor Rachel, but I was so relieved, I pressed my hand to my mouth to stifle a sob. "The pillowcase, the stab wound—"

"Those are well-known markers of the PTK." His gaze swept over to the wall. "That's not his writing, not his usual message and definitely not his... or her... shade of lipstick."

I looked at him. "You're sure?"

"It's still stamped in my brain as if I was standing in the crime scenes just yesterday. This was not the PTK."

I walked over to the open window. "I doubt anyone would have had an open window last night. Looks like the killer came through this way."

Nate joined me at the window. "But where are the footprints, the debris, the melted puddles of snow? The floor looks clean under the window."

Nate was right. I sucked in a breath. "So, the killer was already in the house?"

Nate shrugged. "Unless he came to the door, and the victim let him in. The killer might have left through the window. That would still leave a clean floor. I think we'd better talk to the other women. Nothing about any of this is adding up."

nine

I FOLLOWED Nate back to Sera's. Even trudging through the snow, he walked with confidence and purpose. It seemed I was getting a glance of Detective Nathaniel Maddon, and I liked it. He looked dashing and serious and even more appealing than usual, and that was saying a lot. Then, a streak of worry smashed my moment of adoration. Would this case make him miss his badge? It was a constant source of concern for me. It seemed inevitable that Nate would eventually tire of island life and return to the excitement of the city. I'd known a few people who'd tried to make an island-mainland relationship work, but eventually, they all came to the same heartbreaking end.

Sera came to the door and stepped out onto the stoop. This time she'd pulled on a coat. "You'll need to give them a little more time," Sera said. "Toni has finally stopped throwing up, and Betsy and Ariel are sobbing in between arguing about who will have to notify Rachel's husband."

"Tell them to hold off on notifying next of kin," Nate said. "Let's get a better handle on all this first. Hopefully by then, the harbor will have quieted down enough to get law enforcement to the island." Nate put up his hand to stop our laughter. "I know, Norwich is a moron, but he should be the one to notify next of kin. It shouldn't fall to any of the women, and if one of those women—" He didn't finish his sentence.

Sera's eyes rounded. "You don't think one of the women killed her?" she whispered. "I hadn't even considered that. I guess that's why you're the professional."

"Ex-professional," I chirped. Nate and Sera looked at me in question. I shrugged. "I mean, obviously, he's the professional, but he's not working for the police anymore." Then I realized why I said it. Something had been irritating me since we arrived at the scene. I was used to being in charge. Nate's navy-blue eyes gazed at me for a second, then the slightest smile tilted his mouth. He could always read my mind. He knew but he didn't say anything in front of Sera.

"So, what they were saying—" Sera started tentatively. "About the Pillow Talk Killer. Even Samuel thought it might be the serial killer. We've both been worried sick about it."

Nate looked at me to answer. It took me a second to realize he was handing over the reins. "Nate knows a lot of undisclosed details about the PTK, and he says it's a copycat murder. But don't let the women know that yet. We need to keep them all in the dark about everything in case one of them is the killer."

50

Nate's nod of approval was so slight, Sera didn't notice. But I did and I had to hold back a grin.

"We'll give the women a little more time to pull themselves together," I said. "But then we'll need to talk to them. Nate and I are going to head back to the Meyer house and search for evidence."

Sera seemed to be figuring out what our new dynamic was about. She smiled at me and winked. "So glad you're here, Anna. Uh, and you, too, Nate."

Nate and I headed back toward the crime scene. I took hold of his arm and squeezed it. "If I haven't mentioned it before—you're a very good boyfriend."

Nate leaned over and kissed the top of my head. "Just a *good* boyfriend, eh?"

"A great boyfriend. Actually—a spectacular boyfriend."

"I'm sorry about stepping on your toes. It's a force of habit I guess I haven't kicked yet. You are the official investigator on Frostfall Island, but I'm here to help if you want it."

"Of course, I want your help. I would have been worried that we were dealing with a serial killer on the island. Your expertise will be greatly appreciated."

Nate tilted his head back toward Sera's house. "I don't know, you were pretty expert back there too, reminding Sera not to give away anything pertinent to the women before we knew more ourselves."

We were facing a grisly crime scene inside, but I couldn't stop a grin. "I guess I've picked up a few skills along the way. I'm going to head around the side of the house to that back window. I want to look for tracks before the snow falls again and covers everything. If you wouldn't mind looking over the crime scene," I added meekly, then laughed. "I'd never make a good captain or chief."

"I think you're wrong there," Nate said. He headed inside. "I'll get some photos too."

I found a path through the snow that was free of any marks or muddy puddles, so I wouldn't create confusion with my own footprints. I reached the rear of the house where Rachel's room was located and found the slightly opened window. Just like there were no signs of an intruder inside the house, the outside snow was clean and untouched. There was a bristly holly shrub just to the left of the window, but the rest of the area below the window was free of shrubs and debris. It was possible the murder happened during the storm; in fact, it was highly likely. Enough precipitation had fallen through the night to cover someone's tracks, although my experience of walking through snow told me there would be at least depressions in the snow that had been previously marred by footprints. The snow leading from the back window was pristine. Nothing had walked this way, not even a bird or squirrel.

Nate leaned down to the window from inside. "Any luck?"

"Either our killer had wings on their shoes or, like you said, they were already in the house."

"Looks like there's a storage shed in the yard," Nate said as he peered through the breath-fogged pane.

I glanced back at the shed. It was more a small garage with a window on one side and gray shingles to match the house. "Should I check inside? Maybe the killer hid in there during the storm," I said as I surveyed the snow. "But again, no footprints. I don't think anyone has been out here since the storm began. Not even any animals."

"It looks very untouched. I was thinking we could move the body out to the shed. It's too warm in the house. It's cold enough in the shed for a makeshift morgue until the coroner can reach the island."

"And that's why I'm glad you're here with me," I said. "That and I really like to hang out with my spectacular boyfriend. Even if he's standing in a room with a dead body." I moved closer to the window and peered inside. "I wonder if we need to do a lipstick check, find the matching shade in someone's handbag."

"I found the lipstick. The killer wrote their message and then threw the lipstick under the bed. I placed it in tissue on the nightstand. The outside of the lipstick container is shiny black acrylic, but I can't see any prints. I guess the storm has cut us off from forensics too. This is going to be a real back-to-basics investigation."

"Not that having Detective Norwich on board makes it any less back-to-basics."

Nate nodded. "That's right. You always do this without forensics. That shows you're a better detective than the rest of us. We usually rely on science for answers, and you're out here relying on your instincts and intuition."

"Yes, and my intuition is telling me my nose is going to break off from the cold if I don't get inside soon. The sky doesn't look too friendly, either." The second I said it, small flakes started falling. "See what I mean."

"I'll get Samuel to help me move the body while you talk to the women."

"Good plan." I used my same footprints and hurried to the front of the house. I'd noticed a yearbook sitting open on the coffee table amongst the empty wine glasses, melted candles and snack bowls. It was open to a page. I stuck a napkin on the page to save the place.

Nate came out of the hallway. He smiled proudly. "I was going to tell you that an old yearbook sometimes holds dark secrets."

I thought about Michael's high school girlfriend who had shown up at our wedding, uninvited. Her handwritten note to Michael in his yearbook further deepened the mystery around Denise Fengarten. I was sure she was the one holding the twins in the photo. "Trust me, Nate, no one knows about yearbook secrets more than me." He knew exactly what I was talking about and seemed sorry he'd made the statement at all. "Are you coming along? I hope Sam is up to the task. Sera was stunned at how shaken he was this morning."

"If you're not used to seeing murder victims it can take some time to recuperate. I'm sure he can help. I took a lot of photos so Norwich doesn't have a fit when he finds we've moved the body."

Nate was right. The house was warm. "We can't possibly leave her here. If Sam isn't up to the task, I can help." I smiled over at him as we left the house. "*Partner*."

ten

NATE AND SAMUEL had the unenviable job of moving Rachel's body to the shed for cold storage. I had an equally unenviable job of sitting down to talk with a group of highly distressed women, and they all looked equally distraught. It was hard to find even one expression or mannerism in the group that pointed out a possible killer.

"I was hoping to talk to each of you about last night," I said feeling unusually uncomfortable about the suggestion. All three women stared up at me from behind tissues and puffy eyes.

"I don't understand." The platinum blonde who'd argued with Rachel about the bunk bed tugged her sweater and sat up straighter. "Are you with the police?"

She was just condescending enough that I found some backbone. "My name is Anna St. James. I'm the closest thing you've got to police unless you want me to walk away. Then I'll tell Nate and Sam to leave Rachel in the room, and the three of you can sit in the house and wait for the storm to allow safe passage across the harbor. Might be a day or two but I'm sure it'll be fine. However, I can't guarantee the power will stay on for the duration."

The blonde crumpled from her defensive posture. "What is it you want to know?"

"First of all, I have this yearbook." I held it up to three surprised faces.

"What do you need with that?" Toni, the woman who gave up her bedroom, asked. It seemed her generosity might have saved her life.

"Nothing really. I just wanted to get a better picture of your friendship and relationships." I sat in the chair opposite the couch and opened it to the napkin marked page.

The woman with braids laughed harshly. "You can't possibly think it was one of us. Unless you've been off the planet—" She smiled demurely. "Which in a way you have. Rachel was clearly attacked by that awful serial killer. Surely, word about the Pillow Talk Killer has reached this remote little island."

"Yes, it has," I said curtly. "I can't tell you how I know this, but the murder was not committed by the Pillow Talk Killer."

"But you're not the real police," the woman said. "How would you know that for sure?"

"You'll just have to trust me." I glanced at a yearbook photo on the marked page. There were five girls standing in a row with big, young smiles and arms looped together. Years had passed, but it was still easy to recognize the faces. I looked up at the red-haired woman. She looked just as sporty in high school and happened to be wearing a softball uniform in the photo. "According to the caption below this picture—you're Betsy Archer. Is that still your name?"

She looked hesitant to answer at first, then nodded. "Yes, I was married for two years and then went back to my maiden name after the divorce."

"You played softball?" I asked. I had no real plan for this interview, but I was trying to break the ice with small talk. I was sensing a lot of hesitation coming from the trio on the couch.

"Yes, I was pitcher and pretty darn good," she said with a humble shrug.

"Pretty darn good?" Toni asked and turned to me. "She got a full scholarship based on her skills."

"Wonderful," I said. "Where did you attend college?"

Toni dropped her face; apparently sorry she'd brought it up.

"I hardly think that matters after what's happened," Betsy said.

"Right." I glanced at the yearbook and found Toni. "Toni Margett," I said.

"That's me and it's still Margett. I never married."

"And I'm in the center, the taller one with the blonde hair and cheerleader uniform. It says Ariel Coffman, but I go by Ariel Frasier now, my second husband's name. Rachel is the brunette next to me with the other cheer uniform. We were on the squad together." Her voice wavered. "I still can't believe she's gone. Who could have done something so awful?" Toni put her arm around Ariel's shoulder.

"I'd like to talk to each of you separately." I'd hoped that I broke the ice enough, but I was wrong. Betsy seemed to have appointed herself group spokesman and legal expert.

"Not without lawyers present. Not to mention you don't really have authority to ask us anything." She seemed to recall my earlier warning about leaving them on their own until it was safe to cross the harbor, something that wasn't happening soon considering the newly reenergized wind and snow outside. She shrank back, more contrite. "Whatever you want to ask, we'd prefer if you asked it in a group." The other women nodded in agreement.

I'd hoped since we were all women of approximately the same age, I could gain their trust. That wasn't the case. They were on a strange island, seemingly cut off from the world for at least the next day, and now one of their friends had been brutally murdered. They couldn't trust anyone.

"That's fine. I understand completely. Maybe one of you could give me a quick recap of last night and this morning's events."

The other two looked toward Betsy. She straightened. "We all drank some wine and snacked on junk food. It was a very nice evening, despite the terrible weather. The fire and candles provided plenty of warmth and light, so we talked and laughed for hours. We reminisced about high school." She motioned toward the yearbook.

I glanced down at the photo again and realized there was one face in the photo that wasn't in the room... or in the shed. "Who is—" I slid my finger along the caption. "Who is Carla Sanders?"

"I think her name is Overton now," Toni spoke up. "We didn't really keep in touch with her much. She—she—" Toni didn't know how to finish.

"Oh, you know how sometimes friendships dissolve after high school," Ariel said. "Carla went her own way."

"You were saying—" I returned to the previous topic.

Betsy continued. "I think we all went to bed around one. Rachel was the first person to turn in. She always fell asleep first at our slumber parties too," she said with a smile toward her friends. Then her expression turned grim. "I can't believe this has happened. Anyhow, I woke up around six. I'm an early riser. The power wasn't on yet, so I lit some more candles and set to work making peanut butter and jelly sandwiches. I figured that would be the best we could do for breakfast. Then, let me see—" She looked at her friends.

Toni nodded. "I came out next and started helping you with the sandwiches."

Ariel took a deep, steadying breath. Toni once again comforted her by patting her leg. "I woke up and got out of bed. I saw Toni and Betsy already making breakfast, so I pulled on my robe and washed up. I knocked on Rachel's door to let her know the bathroom was free, but there was no answer. I knocked louder and still no answer. I walked out and asked the girls if Rachel had gone out? I thought it was strange because the weather outside was so bad. Neither of them had seen her. That's when I noticed her coat and scarf were still on the hook. I hurried back to the bedroom and knocked again. No answer. I opened the door." She lowered her face into her hands and sobbed.

"As you can see, Ms. St. James," Betsy said curtly. "We're all in a great deal of distress right now. I'm sure you can understand why we'd like to be left alone for a bit. We're all grieving the loss of a dear friend."

I nodded. "Right. I'll leave you for now." The storm outside the window seemed to be gaining steam. "Rachel's body has been moved to the storage shed on the property. If the body was left inside the warm house... I'm sure I don't need to elaborate. There's a hotel on the island if you're not comfortable staying in the house. If you do decide to stay in the rental, I suggest checking that all the doors and windows are locked."

"Is that how the murderer got inside?" Toni asked.

"I don't know that for certain."

"Otherwise, they would have come through the front door, and I know I locked that door," Toni said.

Her comment caught my attention, and it gave me a quick opening, which I was glad to take no matter how brief. "You're sure it was locked?"

"Absolutely."

"Is there any reason Rachel would have gotten up to let someone inside?" I asked.

They looked at each other and were shaking their heads before Ariel spoke up. "With that storm churning outside? Why on earth would she have done that?"

I nodded. "Yes, it doesn't make much sense."

"Some crazy person must have been lurking around the island, and they found an unlocked window," Betsy said. "We'll have to be more diligent tonight."

Ariel looked at Betsy. "Do you think we should stay in the house?"

"We paid for the darn place. Like Ms. St. James said, we'll double check to make sure everything is locked."

I glanced out the window and saw Nate and Samuel heading back to the house. I stood up. "Thank you for your time, and if any of you think of something that might help once the police get to the island, let me know."

Sera had heard most of the conversation from her kitchen. She shrugged at me as I walked to the front door. This was going to be tough one, even with Norwich out of the way.

eleven

NATE SEEMED to be deep in thought as we walked back across to the Meyer house. "My partner seems to be sorting some things out," I said hopefully. "And that's a good thing because I can tell you my interview with the women was an utter flop."

"I think we should look a little harder for the murder weapon. I'll check the kitchen knives. Maybe the killer got sloppy with cleanup. It was a brutal stabbing, and while we don't have a warrant to search their personal things, the kitchen utensils belong with the house."

"Good idea." I stopped and swept my eyes around the front of the house.

Nate looked back. "Do you see something?"

"I was focused on the rear of the property because of that window. The front path to the doorway was already trampled by the women and Samuel. If the killer just sauntered up to the front door, there would be no way to find his or her footprints. I can only assume the killer didn't fly in and land right at the start of the path. There are a lot of prints going back and forth between Sera's house and the rental house. Ours are there too. But—" My eyes swept toward the road. "There." I pointed excitedly. "I can see the path we took and our prints, but there's another set of prints on the road. We didn't notice them on the way in."

I hurried over to where the road met the walkway to the door. The snow was mostly a sludgy, icy mess from everyone going back and forth, but one set of prints was farther out and clear of the already trampled snow. They were mere indentations and not terribly clear because the storm had erased most of the prints. Nate was behind me, but he stood back and let me do my sleuthing thing. I pulled out my phone to get a photo of the prints before they were covered by the new falling snow.

"Small boots and a pole?" I said the last part as a question because the impression left in the snow looked more like the rubber end on a crutch or cane and not the usual small hole left by ski or trekking poles. I walked across to the prints Nate and I had made as we walked down the road. My poles left distinct holes all the way down to the road itself. The round marks that accompanied the mostly erased prints were much bigger.

"Doesn't look like a pole," Nate said. "A cane, maybe?"

"Something like that. Or possibly a walking stick with a big rubber end. Regardless, Sera's house is at the end of the cul-de-sac. Who else would walk down here in the middle of a storm? I think this proves that someone was outside the house last night."

"I agree. The tracks seem to end near the walkway. The rest of their prints must have gotten trampled by all our footsteps."

"It looks like the person walked away on the far side of the road. The trees are heavier on this side. Maybe they were trying to avoid the wind."

"So, we know someone walked toward the house and then walked away from the house," Nate said. "But who? What if it was one of the women in the house?"

"They gave me a quick recap of the evening. It went exactly how you'd expect, talking, sipping wine and reminiscing about the past. There was no mention of anybody going out for a walk. And who'd do that in a storm?"

"Right." Nate squinted up at the light flakes falling from the dark sky. "You got pictures of the prints, right? Looks like we're going to get a lot more precipitation today."

I patted the phone in my pocket. "Got everything I need. Let's look for the murder weapon. I have an idea where it might be."

"Do you?" he said, sounding impressed. "Sure could have used a partner like you back in town."

"And I could have made you delicious lunches too," I added.

"Not to mention the occasional kiss and hug. Sounds like every detective's dream partner."

We headed back to the house, but I didn't go inside. "I'm

going to check around the back once more while you inspect the kitchen knives."

"Aye, aye, Cap'n. See, you'd make a great captain."

I waved off his comment and found my old tracks to the back of the house. I double checked for more of the tracks I found on the road but couldn't see any depressions or disturbances in the snow. The flakes that were falling were still light like powder, but I was sure they were just a precursor to bigger, heavier and wetter snowfall. I reached the back window. The holly shrub to the left of the window was close enough that someone could have tossed the murder weapon into it, and since the plant was an evergreen, it retained a lot of foliage—pokey foliage, I thought as I moved aside some of the branches. The tiny sharp points on the leaves tried hard to puncture my gloves. I pushed aside a few branches but no luck. I moved in front of the window and reenacted throwing something toward the bush. If I flung a heavy object hard enough, it might miss the shrub altogether, or it might land in a thin area of branches and fall all the way through to the ground. I circled around the shrub and found both my theories were close. A black handle stuck out of the snow that had accumulated under the shrub. The object had nearly cleared the entire shrub, but it landed in the sparser edge of branches and then fell to the ground.

I crouched down near the handle. My gloves were doing two jobs today—keeping my fingers from freezing and allowing me to pick up evidence with care and without adding fingerprints. I pushed aside the prickly branches and pulled the handle free. Just as I expected, a long, sharp blade followed. It left behind blood-stained snow. I pinched it between two fingers and hurried to the house.

Nate had seen me through the front window. He opened the front door. "You are a genius. Where'd you find it?"

"There was a large holly shrub just left of the opened window. Maybe that was why the window was open. The killer tossed it into the bush." I carried it in the same manner to the kitchen. Nate grabbed a kitchen towel and placed it on the tile counter. I set the knife down and followed up with some photos.

"Yep, I'd say no question that it's the murder weapon," Nate said.

"When I pulled the blade free of the snow, it left behind some traces of blood."

"If you wanted to stab someone to death with one good blow, this long, serrated blade would do the trick."

"It reminds me of my sourdough cutting knife." I looked into the kitchen. There was a wooden block with knife handles jutting out. The handles were polished wood, and every slot in the wood block was filled.

"Didn't come from the set," Nate said. "There aren't any knives missing, and the handle is different. There were a few miscellaneous knives in a rack in the drawer by the stove, but same thing, each slot has a knife."

"This could still have come from the kitchen." I blew a frustrated puff of air from my lips. "I thought finding the murder weapon was going to give us a little more to go on, but we're still in the same spot. Someone either outside or inside the house killed Rachel. And the knife was either carried here by the killer or it was found somewhere in this kitchen. The Meyers might be more help with that." I looked at Nate. "Gosh, wait until they hear that their sweet little beach house, the star of the Frostfall vacation rentals, has been tainted by murder. Something tells me their long waiting list is going to shrink to nothing."

"Or it might get longer," Nate suggested. "People are weird." He wrapped the kitchen towel around the knife. I'm going to put this in the crime scene room. I'm sure the women won't be going in there tonight."

"I don't know about you, but all this murder stuff is making me hungry. Let's go check on the women at Sera's and then head home for lunch."

"Sounds like a plan, boss," he quipped.

"Boss, eh? A girl could get used to that."

twelve

SERA HAD MADE sandwiches and tea for her three stunned and unexpected houseguests. They sat at Sera's table nibbling the sandwiches. There was very little conversation. Sera motioned for us to follow her to the living room. Samuel was there in an easy chair eating a sandwich.

"Nate," he said excitedly, nearly dumping the plate on his lap. "How's it going? I've never seen anything like it, someone stabbed to death in their bed." Samuel set the plate on the coffee table. "Did you guys find anything? I have to say Sera and I were holed up in this room all night, sleeping by the fire. The drapes were drawn, and I only looked out once to make sure a particularly big streak of lightning hadn't struck the trees or the house. The road was empty at that time but then I didn't expect to see anything but the storm."

"That reminds me," I said. Samuel was extremely fond of Nate and held him in high regard, so naturally, he directed his comments and questions toward his friend. I had

Samuel's attention now. "Is there a neighbor on this road who likes to take a walk around the cul-de-sac? Someone who walks with a cane or a walking stick or some sort of walking aid?"

Sam and Sera looked at each other, but both were shaking their heads. "Some of the neighbors walk their dogs down here to the end of the road and then circle back the other way, but I can't think of anyone who walks with a cane or stick. I'm sure no one was out last night. Those winds were brutal," Sera said. "Why do you ask? Do you think it was someone who lives on this street?"

"No, I'm sure that's not the case." I lowered my voice. The house was small enough that our voices could carry into the kitchen. "Have they said anything to you at all? Anything that might help the case? They weren't very forthcoming with me."

Sera moved closer to me. "They were pretty tight-lipped when I asked if they had any idea how this might have happened, but I think that's mostly because they're in shock. However, when I was fixing them their sandwiches, they were talking, and Ariel seemed a little miffed at Betsy. She was angry that Betsy took charge of everything this morning, and Ariel thought they should have been more open to the nice *Ms. St. James* because she was only trying to help."

"How did Betsy take the criticism?" I asked.

"Betsy snapped back and told her she was only trying to do what was best for all of them. Toni piped up too. She seems to be the quiet, more reserved one of the bunch. In fact, it's hard to see how she fits in with the rest."

"I told you, sweetie," Samuel said. "She's the rich girl. Two were cheerleaders, one was the star athlete and the quiet one was tolerated because she was from a rich family. I knew a group of girls just like them in high school. They sort of ruled the hallways, if you know what I mean."

I looked at Sera. She shrugged. "He might be right. Toni is wearing a platinum and diamond watch that looks a lot like the one Cora wears."

"What did Toni say in reaction to Ariel's criticism toward Betsy?" I asked.

"She told her friends they were just upset, and they shouldn't take it out on each other. She seems to be the mediator of the group. Just like when she gave Rachel her room because Rachel didn't want the top bunk. That was a big mistake." Sera's mouth dropped open. "Maybe the wrong person was killed. Maybe that knife was meant for Toni."

I glanced toward Nate and he nodded. "Definitely something to keep in mind. If we're looking for possible motives, then we need to look at suspects who might also have wanted to kill Toni. If she's rich, based on the watch," he said skeptically, "then money might be a motive. Maybe someone stands to inherit a lot of money from Toni. Whoever it was, they had a plan. They came to the murder well-equipped to make it look like the work of the PTK. Which reminds me—we should ask them about the lipstick color on the wall. I took a picture of the actual lipstick." Nate handed me his phone. "This is your case, captain. And don't mention the PTK. The lipstick color is a detail that's not widely known."

"My lips will be sealed about *lipstick*," I quipped. "Oh boy, I must be getting lightheaded for lunch."

"I can make you both a sandwich," Sera said.

"Thanks, Sera, but I need to feed my crew at home too. They're probably getting grumpy waiting for lunch."

I walked into the kitchen. The women looked up. No one was pleased to see me. "Sorry to interrupt your lunch, but I need you guys to look at this lipstick. I promise there's nothing horrifying in the picture." I showed them each the dark pink lipstick in the black acrylic holder.

"That's Rachel's color," Ariel said. "Passion Pink and that's her brand too."

The others nodded along. "Yes, she was wearing it yesterday, and I asked her what the name of the color was," Betsy said. "Although, as a red-head, I usually stick with the red shades."

I closed the photo. "That answers my question."

"I thought the PTK always wrote messages in lipstick," Toni said. "How can we be sure it wasn't the serial killer?"

"I can't tell you how I know, but this was not the PTK. We're going to head home for now. On my way, I'll check the harbor and text the ferry captain to see if there's any news on the boat running again. In the meantime, lock up windows and doors, and I'm sure I don't need to say it, but stay out of the room. The police will have to dust for prints and other evidence, and we don't want to contaminate the crime scene. Are you sure you won't be more comfortable in the hotel?"

Before the other two could answer, Betsy spoke up. "We paid a lot of money for that house—"

"Betsy, I told you, I don't mind renting us some rooms. I'll gladly pay for it," Toni said. It seemed Samuel's theory that Toni was the rich friend might be right.

Betsy sighed. "We'll think about it, but for now, we're sticking around here. If the killer does return, I'm going to be ready for him," she said confidently.

Unfortunately, her two friends weren't feeling quite as vengeful or courageous. "Let's hope he doesn't return, Betsy," Ariel said. "I just want to get the heck off this island." She slumped with a frown. "We were all looking so forward to this weekend." She shook her head and sobbed into her napkin.

"I'm sorry this turned out so badly for your celebration. Sera has my number if you need me." Another idea hit me before I left the room. I needed to get to know the women better. I needed to know the dynamics of their relationships better than relying on Samuel's theories based on his high school friends. "I own the Victorian house on Moon River, and I made a ton of food in preparation for the storm. Why don't the three of you walk over around six. It'll be a hot meal and a chance to relax after your harrowing morning."

Their hesitation seemed to indicate they'd turn down my offer. Betsy spoke up first, of course. "That would be nice. And it's very kind of you considering how rudely I acted toward you earlier." She looked at the other two for approval first. It seemed the shock was finally wearing off, and Betsy was acting far less bossy and defensive.

Toni smiled at me. "That would be lovely."

"I'll see you later, then." I walked out.

Nate was waiting for me at the door. We stepped outside, and Sera shut the door behind us. "Any luck with the lipstick?" Nate asked.

"They said it was Rachel's color—Passion Pink. The killer used Rachel's own lipstick to write the message." The snow was falling faster, and the wind was picking up. "I also invited our three main suspects to dinner at the boarding house. I think casual conversation and breaking the ice with good food might give me more insight into their friendships."

"Clever move," Nate said. "Get them drunk on delicious food and baked goods and before you know it, one of them is confessing or they're turning on one another."

"I was just hoping to find out a little more about their high school days and the current status of their friendships, but sure, that works, too. That reminds me." I pulled out my phone and sent off a text to Frannie asking when the ferry would run again. She wrote right back.

"We won't have clearance to cross the harbor for the rest of the day," Frannie said. "Why? Who needs to get to the mainland?"

"No one, but I need Norwich to come to the island," I texted back.

"Oh no, not again."

"Yes, I'm afraid so," I replied.

thirteen

THE STORM HAD A SHORT TEMPER. One minute, things seemed to be calming down and the sky looked more promising, and the next, a fierce wind raced across the island bringing with it ice and snow. The power was as fickle as the weather. It sputtered on and off until it finally chose off just as the five of us sat down to a late lunch of egg salad sandwiches and vegetable soup. Fortunately, the food was ready, so we had a nice candlelit lunch.

The power returned as Cora and I finished doing the dishes. "Oh good, now I can get out the corkboards."

Nate sat at the table drinking coffee and snacking on the ginger cookies. "Uh, did you forget who you invited for dinner? The same people who will be on the corkboard."

"That's true. I guess that might make for awkward dinner conversation. I'll move them before the guests arrive."

Cora lowered her dish drying towel. "Do you mean to tell me we're going to sit down to dinner with a killer? I talked to

Sera earlier. She said the murder was so gruesome, Samuel nearly passed out."

Nate laughed. "Is there such thing as nearly passing out? Either you pass out or you don't. I think Sera might be exaggerating. Samuel helped me move the body."

Cora's chin dropped. "Move the body? Why did you do that?"

"Because the house was too warm," I said with a pointed look. Cora crinkled up her nose when she figured out my meaning. "Anyhow, I'll be putting up the corkboards once we're through with the dishes. Nate, why don't you go into the office and print the photos we took. But let's leave off the particularly gory one of Rachel in the bed. We already know where she died and probably don't need to display it."

"Yes, boss," he said and got up from the table.

Cora laughed. "Did you just call her *boss*?"

I looked over at her. "What's wrong with that? This isn't the 1950s."

Cora held in a teasing grin. "Nothing wrong with it at all."

Nate returned with the photos as we finished up. Cora wasn't in the mood to talk about a murder, but Opal and Tobias joined us in the kitchen. I pulled out my stack of colorful index cards and a pen.

Tobias stacked his hands on the table. "So, what have we got? I've been cooped up in this house, and I've missed out on all the gossip and details." Tobias's accounting office was on the boardwalk in the middle of town. He was always privy to all the noteworthy events, but the storm had cut him off from his usual chain of gossip.

"I'll give you both a quick rundown. Four women came to the island for the weekend for a reunion. They went to high school together."

"It's the friend they tolerated but never fully embraced," Opal said with a confident head nod. Opal had been a teacher, and she knew the dynamics of school friendships well. We waited for her to elaborate. She wasn't expecting our full attention, but she got it. She smoothed down the collar on her housecoat. "I always observed friendship groups when I was teaching, and there was always one friend who was allowed in because of value, like someone with a nice swimming pool in their yard or with rich parents who didn't mind kids hanging out at their big house."

I glanced at Nate. "Guess that would be Toni, so Sam was right." I turned back to Opal. She was loving this.

"Occasionally, that friend was someone whose parent was head of the PTA or whose dad didn't mind carting everyone around on the weekend. Someone who was part of the group but always kind of the—the last person picked for the team. That's the best way I can describe it."

"I wonder who that would be?" I looked at Nate because he was the only person at the table who'd met all the women.

"I guess that's why you're bringing them here tonight," Nate said. "So you can peel off some of those layers and find out the group dynamics. Opal, you picked that person out as the obvious killer, but I'm going to assume you never actually experienced a murder at your high school."

Opal had been sitting taller, happy that she'd offered a theory, but now she slumped a bit. "No murder. I just always felt bad for those kids, the ones who'd follow the group around like a stray puppy and only occasionally get a pat on the head." She picked up another cookie. "Motive maybe?"

Nate nodded. "Can't rule it out."

"These women are my age. That's a long time to hold a grudge about not being treated as well as the others, but I suppose if the others were particularly pernicious to the person, then it's possible. That's why I need to know more about Rachel. She and Ariel were cheerleaders at the school—"

Opal groaned. "Cheerleaders. I knew a few mean ones, that's for sure."

This visit back to the hallowed halls of Opal's teaching days wasn't moving the case forward enough. Friendship dynamics could very well play a big part in the motive, but at the moment, we knew very little about the women. I picked up the first index card to write down the victim's name and details. "Rachel was killed in the bed, stabbed with a long, serrated blade." I pinned the card to the corkboard. Nate handed over the photo of the knife to pin next to it.

"Sounds dreadful," Tobias said. "Almost like a PTK murder."

"That's exactly right, Toby. The killer even covered her head with a pillowcase and wrote a message in lipstick."

Opal gasped. "My goodness, do you mean to tell me the PTK is here on Frostfall?"

"It wasn't the PTK," Nate said in a way that told them he wasn't going to elaborate. For months, I was the only person in the house who knew that Nate had been a detective and that he'd turned in his badge because he couldn't catch the PTK. But slowly, as he warmed up to everyone and they warmed up to him, he revealed his reason for moving to the island.

"Yes, let's continue." I picked up another card, a pink one, and wrote down the name Betsy Archer. "Betsy Archer seems to have put herself in charge of the group. It's hard to know if she's replacing Rachel as leader or if she was always the leader, but at least one of the women, Ariel Frasier, wasn't pleased with Betsy taking over. I picked up a blue card for Ariel. "Sera and I witnessed Ariel arguing with the victim yesterday morning about a top bunk bed. Apparently, they'd drawn straws, so to speak, and Rachel ended up on the top bunk. I doubt the argument led to murder especially because it was quickly resolved when Toni Margett offered to switch beds with Rachel."

Tobias sat up straighter. "Then maybe the wrong person was in the wrong bed when the killer arrived."

I smiled at Tobias. "Gold star for Toby today. Exactly." I picked up a yellow card for Toni. "I'll add on here that she might have been the intended victim."

"Or maybe Toni is the killer and she generously offered the bed because she knew it would be impossible to kill someone on a top bunk, especially with someone sleeping below," Opal said.

I looked at Nate. His eyes were as round as mine. Neither of us had thought of that possibility.

"And Opal gets a gold star too," I said.

"I'd prefer a second cookie." She picked up a cookie. Tobias did the same.

"You guys are getting really good at this," I said as I pinned on the last card. "Now if you could put those gold star heads together and tell me who did this, that would be great. Might even offer an extra recess."

Tobias stretched up to look out through the kitchen window. "You can keep the extra recess. It's snowing again."

"Maybe your suspects won't make it to dinner after all," Nate said.

"I guess that's possible." I pulled one more card out of the pack, a white one.

"What's the white card for?" Tobias asked.

I put a big question mark in the middle of the card and held it up. "It's for our mystery suspect. One who may or may not exist." A streak of lightning lit up the kitchen. Huck sat up and scurried over to sit next to Nate. A loud clap of thunder followed. "And this storm isn't going to make the case any easier."

fourteen

THE WEATHER CALMED ENOUGH that my three guests showed up at the door looking weary, stressed and hungry. They were more than pleased to sit down to a nice hot meal. I warmed up the chili and baked the cheesy potatoes. I tossed together a big salad, and there were frosted brownies for dessert.

My kitchen table was big enough to accommodate everyone with room to spare. I purposely separated the women, hoping Betsy would have less control of the conversation if Toni and Ariel were sitting between my Moon River family members. I made sure to put Toni next to Cora, and since their conversation went straight to their nearly identical diamond watches and how Tiffany watches were always the best, I knew I'd made the right decision. My sister had grown up with very little, like me, but she could pretend to be from the ultra-rich class as if she grew up with the Vanderbilts and Rockefellers.

Betsy had grabbed my interest more than the others mostly because of her brusque attitude when we first met. She'd made up for that some when I spoke to the women over their sandwiches, but she still stood out from the rest. "Betsy was a softball player in high school," I said to Opal who sat next to her. Not that Opal had any particular interest in softball, but I needed to get the conversation going. "And Ariel was a cheerleader, right?" I said to Ariel on Opal's other side.

Ariel wiped her mouth. "That's right." She took a sip of her water. "Rachel was the captain of the cheer squad, and I was co-captain." She smiled. "Those were the days. So much fun riding to games with the football team. Betsy had wanted to join us on the squad, but she didn't make the final cut. Rachel and Ms. Harrington, the cheer teacher, didn't think she had the gymnastic and dancing skills needed." Ariel leaned forward. "Do you still have two left feet, Betsy?" Ariel asked with a laugh.

I sensed tension coming from Betsy even though she smiled back. Opal was wedged between them and was giving me a secret look. She must have sensed it too.

"I really didn't have my heart in cheerleading. I always thought it was silly," Betsy said.

Ariel didn't seem to take offense. "Rachel not picking you for the squad was the best thing that could have happened. You went on to become the star of the softball team."

"That's right. You mentioned you got a full scholarship," I said. Earlier when I'd asked about her college years, I was abruptly cut off.

"This chili is delicious," Betsy said. It seemed I was being cut off again, and this time, by my own chili.

"Thanks," I said. "How long have all of you been friends? Was it since high school?"

Toni had tired of trading rich girl opinions with Cora. She joined in our conversation. "Ariel and Rachel have been friends since junior high." Her expression turned grim. "Poor Rachel," she said softly.

"I became friends with them on the first day of high school," Betsy said. "Two middle schools merged into one high school. Toni and I came from the other school." She leaned forward to address Toni. "Toni, when did you start hanging out with us?"

"After the first dance our freshman year," Toni said.

Betsy laughed. "That's right. Your dad paid for the school to hire a live band, one of the best ones in the area."

"That made you pretty darn popular," Ariel added.

It was a snide thing to say, and Toni felt the sting of it. It seemed Samuel had been right about Toni.

Toni leaned forward to address Ariel. "I can't believe you and Rachel stayed such close friends after Rachel stole your boyfriend." It was a comment I never would have expected from Toni, but something told me hanging out with this group taught her how to play offense as well as defense.

Cora was stuck between the two women. She flashed me a scowl. My crew were starting to look a little uncomfortable with their buffer positions.

"She didn't steal him. I'd already moved on to Darren Jacobson. Oscar and I were long over."

Betsy looked at her with wide eyes. "Gee, then what was the big scene in the hallway in front of the lockers where you slapped Oscar and then called Rachel—well, I won't say it at the dinner table."

I shot a quick peek in Nate's direction. He stared back at me with no particular expression. He didn't need one. I knew we were both thinking the same thing. This dinner had helped peel back some important layers.

"Let's not talk about Rachel like this." Ariel picked up her napkin to blot her eyes. "It's wrong. Our lovely friend is inside a cold storage shed waiting for a coroner to take her away. And poor Ryan. Who is going to tell Ryan that Rachel is gone?" This new turn in conversation caused awkward silence at the table as the three women sobbed into their napkins. I was getting some very annoyed scowls from my housemates.

"I'd wait until tomorrow before making any calls," Nate said. "I was reading about the weather, and it seems the worst part of the storm has passed. There's a good chance the police will be able to get to the island tomorrow, and they will handle notifying next of kin."

I'd noticed more than once that Betsy got twinkles in her eyes whenever she looked at Nate. She smiled his direction. "When you talk, you sound as if you worked in law enforcement."

Nate shrugged. "Just a guy who helps restore lighthouses."

"Well, I don't want to be too forward, but it would sure be nice if you saw us home after dinner," Betsy said to Nate.

"And if you wouldn't mind checking the locks on the doors and windows." Nothing about Betsy made her seem like the type who ever liked to be the damsel in distress. She even mentioned staying at the house, so she could personally confront the killer if they returned. But she was putting on a good show this evening.

Nate nodded and looked at me. "Would that be all right with you, *sweetie?*" He never used that term, but it gave Betsy the message. Her posture deflated some.

"I think that's a great idea, *dear*," I said. "But first, I have fudge brownies, and I'm sure everyone could use a cup of hot tea."

fifteen

HUCK'S small whine was followed by him placing his chin on my chest. Most of the time the dog preferred to sleep on his pillow on the bedroom floor, but thunder and lightning always turned my otherwise confident and extroverted dog into a scared little bunny. He crawled into the bed with me and snuggled closer with each clap of thunder. This morning I woke up on a six-inch slice of the mattress just one good, sleepy roll away from falling on the floor. Huck was sprawled out across the entire mattress. Now that the thunder was gone, he'd decided it was time for a walk.

I smoothed my palm over the top of his head. "I suppose we could do a short hike before the others wake up."

Huck hopped to his feet and flew off the bed. His tail wagged wildly as he waited for me to get ready. The house was quiet as we headed down the stairs. The night before, Nate had walked the women home, then he made sure the house was secure. He suggested that they take shifts staying awake, and he gave them both our phone numbers in case there was trouble. At dinner, we'd learned a few more details about their high school relationships. Once they'd left for the night, I pulled out the corkboards and added the news about Rachel stealing Ariel's boyfriend. I also added that Toni was upset when Ariel and Betsy brought up that her family's money was the reason for her popularity in school. It seemed Betsy had tried out for cheerleading, but she didn't make the cut, and Rachel had been involved in that decision. They all seemed like trivial motives since they happened back in high school, but I had nothing else to go on at the moment.

Huck and I stepped out the back door, and it was as if the house had been picked up and moved to another planet. A regular storm covered the island with a blanket of blinding white snow, but this storm had been so violent shrubs had been uprooted and tree branches were snapped off. The dark clouds had left, and the dawn was smoky pink, a mixture of leftover clouds and sun.

The one thing that hadn't left with the clouds was the cold. And with the island covered in snow and ice, it felt as if Huck and I were hiking through the Arctic. He pranced ahead quickly, but it wasn't out of enthusiasm for the walk. It was because his paws were cold. I'd purchased adorable blue snow boots for his paws a few years back. I put them on his front paws to see how they fit, and Huck walked around the kitchen like a high-stepping circus horse. It was as if he was a newborn just learning to walk. I couldn't stop laughing. The boots went back into the box, never to be seen or spoken of again.

I dropped my face lower to shield it from the cold. I'd left the spikes on my boots, and they helped me hike along the trail at a good pace. We wouldn't be out long, and I was sure my trail partner was fine with that. We reached Olive's cottage. It was early but the fireplace glowed inside. She'd most likely slept in her living room to keep warm. The power stayed on all night, but it sputtered off and on more than once.

Huck's tail wagged as he trotted toward her house with his nose twitching in the air. "No treats this morning, Huck. We're turning around here." Then I saw what had grabbed his attention. He stopped a few feet from Olive's peanut tray. It was empty and a disappointed squirrel was sitting in the middle of the tray. It was Charlie. He immediately began chattering and scolding Huck. Huck wagged his tail a few more seconds, then dropped his head. His tail dropped too.

"Well, I guess you've met your match in the squirrel world," I patted his head. "Let's go home before we both get frostbite." We turned back toward the trail. I still had my face down to avoid the cold. That was when I noticed some impressions in the snow leading away from Olive's cottage. Like before, the prints weren't clear because the new snow had erased the edges, but they were footprints and one round print from a cane or walking stick. It couldn't have been coincidence. The prints were made by the same person.

I sucked in the cold air. It hurt my throat. Huck had gone ahead. I whistled for him to come back. He hesitated when he saw I was heading back to the cottage and toward the squirrel. Charlie had given up on thinking peanuts would magically appear in the tray. He leapt off the tray and ran for the nearest tree before I reached the door.

Adrenaline was pumping through me sending my heart ahead of its normal pace. I knocked on Olive's door. "Olive? It's me, Anna. Is everything all right?" I knocked harder and was just about to go into a full panic when she opened the door.

"Olive." My whole body relaxed, but my heart was still pounding. I rarely saw Olive with her hair down, but it hung in long waves around her shoulders. She was wearing a robe over pajamas and fuzzy slippers on her feet.

"Anna, I wasn't expecting you, and it's so early. Is everything all right? Here, come inside. You look upset."

Huck rushed in ahead of me and quickly curled up on the braided rug in front of the fire. I stepped gently into the house and kept my spiked boots on the doormat. Pillows and quilts were piled on the sofa. Johnny's cage was still covered. He wouldn't wake until Olive took the cover off. She said it was her way to keep him quiet until she was ready for his squawks and songs.

"I'm fine, Olive. I let my imagination get the best of me. There were no peanuts in the squirrel tray—"

Olive's hand flew to her mouth. "I forgot to put them in the tray last night. Charlie will be angry." She hurried to her kitchen and pulled a cup of peanuts out of the pantry cupboard.

I was relieved everything was all right. I'd imagined the worst, and it had scared me plenty. "You know him as Charlie, too?" I asked.

"Nate named him, and I think it fits." She stepped outside in the cold. Peanuts clattered into the tray. "Yoo-hoo—Charlie. Sorry it's late." She stepped inside and shivered once. "My gosh, it's cold out there. And what a mess that storm left." Olive smiled in Huck's direction. She hunched forward and lowered her voice. "Huck is a little nervous when it comes to Charlie."

"I noticed." I chuckled. "As a parent, I worry about his self-esteem." We both laughed. "Poor guy. He does manage to terrorize every other small creature on the island, so maybe it's good for him. A little humility never hurt anyone."

"I could make some tea," Olive said.

"No, I need to get back and start breakfast. I'm sorry if I woke you. Aside from the peanuts, there were some footprints out in your yard and I worried—" I stopped. I didn't need to frighten Olive with my tales of murder and mayhem. Not that she was easily frightened.

"Oh, those might have been from last night's visitor."

"Visitor? What visitor?" I tried not to sound frantic, but it was hard. Olive rarely had visitors, and she spoke to very few people on the island, preferring to keep mostly to herself.

"No need to worry, Anna. It was a nice young woman with a camera. I looked out my window just as the sun was setting, and she looked lost. The storm had subsided some, but I was worried so I went to the door and called to her. She was indeed lost, so I invited her in for some tea. She seemed relieved to find a place to take shelter for a bit." Olive rubbed her chin. "Let me see, her name was something with a C. Can't remember, darn it. She said she was visiting the island for the weekend." Olive's face brightened. "She's an artist too, a photographer. She said the storm had given her some beautiful shots."

"Where is she staying?" I asked.

"She said she was staying in a cottage on Island Drive. She was enamored with Johnny, of course, and we mostly talked about art and trying to keep relevant on social media. I told her Johnny was my golden ticket for that, and she laughed and thought she should consider getting a quirky pet. Poor girl walked with a cane. She said it was from an accident when she was a teen. It was obvious she didn't want to talk about it, and I didn't push it."

"A cane," I said to myself. "How long did she stay? Did she mention being here for any other reason, like to see old friends?"

My questions were puzzling Olive. Her brows bunched together. "She was here for about an hour. Then I told her how to get back to Island Drive. I worried the storm would start up again, so I hurried her along. What are you not telling me, Anna? I can always tell when you've got something troubling you."

"There was a murder on the island, Olive." It was a statement that should've made her pause, but she knew too well that our charming little island had more than its share of murders. Opal liked to tease me, telling me the island was cursed.

"Oh dear, just what you needed with this terrible weather. Have you tracked down the killer yet? You don't think it that's nice woman with the cane?"

"No, well, to be honest, I'm not sure. Right now, anyone stuck on this island during the storm is a suspect. I'm hoping the weather will allow Detective Norwich to get to the island."

Olive laughed. "Well, you must be desperate if you're waiting for that ridiculous man to arrive."

"Either way, keep your doors and windows locked, Olive, and be wary of letting strangers into your house." The last part of my admonition produced a scowl.

"Now, Anna, I've been on my own for a long time. I can take care of myself."

I hugged her. "I'm sorry. I didn't mean that to come out so bossy or to insinuate that you needed looking after. I guess this case has me a little shaken."

Olive took my hand. "Then why don't you step back on this one and let that worthless detective earn his keep for a change."

"You know Norwich, he'll just arrest the wrong person. He always makes snap judgements to close the case fast. I'll be fine. I'm determined to figure this out and sooner, rather than later. With any luck, I'll have it solved and wrapped up by the time the toothpick-chewing numbskull reaches the island."

"I hope you're right." We hugged again. Huck was reluctant to leave the cozy fire, but once we stepped outside, he took off at a trot. We were both anxious for breakfast.

sixteen

IT WAS Saturday but it felt as if we'd already had our weekend. The breakfast crowd was grumpy. Cora always complained about having to work, but she was bored when she was off. Opal hadn't slept well because of the lightning and thunder, and Tobias was feeling antsy without his morning swims and time in the office. Nate, on the other hand, was happy not to be standing on scaffolding on the side of the lighthouse. My prediction was that the entire island would be up and running by Monday or Tuesday. In the meantime, I had a murder to solve.

I sat down with another cup of coffee and sent a text to Frannie. "How does it look for a harbor crossing?"

"We're not cleared to start the ferry service yet. Do you want me to call in the emergency so they're aware we're going to need police and a coroner on the first ferry out?"

"That would be great. Thanks so much."

"I'll keep you posted," she wrote back.

My phone rang before I could put it down. I didn't recognize the number. "Hello."

"Hello, is this Anna?" the woman asked urgently.

I sat up straighter. "Yes, this is Anna."

"I'm sorry to bother you. This is Toni from over in the beach house. I wasn't sure who else to call." In the background, someone, Besty, I thought, was talking. "Tell them we've looked everywhere."

"Hello, Toni? Is everything all right?"

"No, it's not. We can't find Ariel. I was still sleeping, and Betsy took a hot bath. She knocked on my door when she realized that Ariel wasn't in her bed. We're very worried. We can't find her anywhere."

"I'll be right over. Stay inside the house and lock the doors."

She sobbed into the phone. "Please hurry."

Nate heard me telling her to stay in and lock doors as he came down the stairs. "Who was that? Did someone else get killed?"

I started pulling on my gear. "Ariel is missing. Toni sounded very upset."

Nate grabbed his coat too. "I'm coming with you."

"I was hoping you would. I don't know why, but I'm feeling off my game with this case. It must be the weather and the fact that my wonderful little island looks torn and injured and sad."

The sun had finally come up, but all it did was highlight the terrible chaos on the island. Nate didn't stop to clear debris this time. If Ariel was missing, then she might be in trouble. We reached the house. Both of us scanned the area for out of place footprints or anything that might help us find Ariel.

"Maybe she's already returned," I said as we reached the door and knocked. "Toni, Betsy, it's Anna and Nate."

Betsy opened the door. Her red hair was piled on top of her head and she smelled perfumy, like bubble bath.

"Did you find her?" I asked as we stepped inside.

"No sign of her," Betsy said. "I looked outside, and I walked over to Sera's house. They haven't seen her either. Toni called her but the phone rang inside her bedroom. She left without it." They'd straightened up the house, and it seemed that suitcases were packed. "We were all hoping to leave here just as soon as the police arrived."

"Only now we can't possibly go without Ariel." Toni was wearing a robe, and she looked far less pulled together than Betsy.

I spotted a pile of colored paper stacked on the coffee table. "Was someone doing crafts?" Betsy's bubble bath seemed strange at a time like this, but a craft session would be even stranger.

"That was Ariel," Toni said. "Ariel makes beautiful things out of paper. It's a hobby. She says it relaxes her, and we certainly all need that this weekend. She was making paper flowers when I went to bed."

Nate looked at me. We both came to the same conclusion. "The shed," I said.

"Yep."

The two women looked puzzled. "Was it possible she was

making some paper flowers to memorialize Rachel? There are no fresh flowers on the island right now."

Toni looked at Betsy. "My gosh, we didn't think of that. I'll bet she's standing out in that shed. She's taking this very hard." Toni looked relieved, but Betsy didn't look convinced.

"She wouldn't be out there. It's freezing cold in that shed." Her words upset Toni, so she changed her tone. "But I'm sure that's where she is. It would be just like Ariel to make paper flowers for Rachel."

Nate and I headed toward the door. He turned back. "Why don't you two stay here—just as a precaution," he added.

Both women were happy to comply. We stepped onto the back stoop. It had been cleared of snow. Yesterday, the snow in the backyard was untouched. This morning it was heavy with footprints, and some areas had been shoveled. The snow shovel was resting against the wall.

"I shoveled some of the snow when I went out to look for Ariel," Besty said.

"Then you already went to the shed," I said. There was a path shoveled all the way to the shed.

Betsy shrugged coyly. "I didn't go inside. I didn't want to see Rachel like that. I guess I should have looked inside for Ariel."

Nate and I used the shoveled path to get to the shed. Nate pulled open the door. Rachel's body had been placed on top of a work table. Paper flowers were lined up around the body. It was dark in the shed. Nate opened the door wider, and that was when we saw her.

Ariel was lying face down on the gritty wood floor of the shed. Her light gray beanie was covered with blood.

Nate hurried over to her and crouched down to take a pulse, but it was obvious she was dead. Her skin was pale blue. "Dead." He used his gloved finger to push up the beanie. "Looks like someone shot her in the back of the head." Nate looked up at me. "Looks like you've got another murder on your hands, Cap'n."

seventeen

NATE TOOK on the grim task of breaking the news to the remaining women. I stood nearby ready with tissues and coffee. The double shock caused Toni to once again rush to the bathroom to throw up. Betsy collapsed onto the couch and dropped her face into her hands.

Four had arrived and now there were only two. Or were there? Something Frannie said had been tapping my brain the whole time. She thought five women had come to the island for the reunion. She based the assumption solely on the fifth woman, one who'd traveled to the island at a different time, seeming the same age and *style* as the others. Purportedly lost, a stranger showed up at Olive's door yesterday afternoon. She was using a cane. There was no doubt in my mind that the same woman had, at one point, walked down Sera's road. Was she just looking for things to photograph, or did she have something to do with the murders?

Nate and I gave the women a few minutes to collect themselves. They were still in a state of shock from Rachel's death, so it seemed they didn't have as far to go to absorb the news.

I sat across from them on the big chair. "Betsy, this morning, when you shoveled the snow on the way to the shed, did you notice any footprints?"

Her eyes were glassy and her nose was red, but she was less distressed than Toni. "I don't think so, but to be honest, I never really looked. I'm not used to the snow, so I didn't even think about looking for footprints."

"Oh, I thought you were from Vermont," I said.

"Rachel and I are from Vermont," Toni interjected. "Ariel lives—" she paused and shook her head, "lived in Rhode Island."

"I live in Texas," Betsy said. "I grew up in Vermont but moved to Texas after high school."

"You *do* have experience with snow then," Nate said. He wasn't trying to be flippant; it was just his natural detective skills coming out.

Betsy lifted her chin defensively. "Obviously, but it's been many years since I lived in it. I didn't think about footprints. And how is this helping? We're obviously sitting ducks in this house." She said it as if we'd forced her to stay at the Meyer place, but she'd insisted on staying.

"Are the police coming soon?" Toni asked. Her hands shook as she wiped her eyes with the tissue. "I'm not sure I'm willing to wait for them anymore. As soon as the ferry is up and running—"

"It should be up and running soon, but I must tell you, I'm certain the police will want to talk to both of you," I said.

"Great, so now we're the suspects." Betsy crossed her arms defensively. "And to think I looked forward to this weekend." She slid a suspicious look toward Toni.

Toni immediately took offense. "You don't think *I* did it? What motive could I possibly have to kill my two closest friends?"

"That's just it. They weren't really your close friends, were they? Ariel and Rachel only welcomed you into the group because you had the massive house, and your dad always paid for our movies and amusement park tickets."

"What about you?" Toni sat forward and pointed. "You were very mad at Rachel for not picking you for the cheerleading squad."

"Don't be ridiculous," Betsy scoffed. "I never wanted to be one of those annoying cheerleaders."

"Of course, you did," Toni replied. "And everyone knows you were the quintessential mean girl in high school. People pretended to like you because they were afraid of you."

I'd let the accusations fly for a few moments hoping something important would come out. I now had more background on the dynamics of their friendships, but it was hard to know if everything they said was being tainted by the heated and harrowing emotions of the moment.

"I think we should step back from the accusations. You're both upset and—"

"Scared witless," Toni said as she pulled her plush robe

tighter around her. It was the first time she'd sounded haughty, and living with my sister, I knew haughty well.

"Exactly," I said. "Now, I have something to ask both of you. When I looked at your yearbook, there was a photo of all of you standing arm in arm. There was a fifth girl in the photo. I can't remember her name, but you said she didn't stay in touch with the group."

I'd brought up a topic that seemed to erase some of the ill will. Betsy nodded knowingly at Toni before she answered. "Carla was one of the hanger-on types. She was always there, even when we hadn't invited her." It was getting easier to see Betsy in her mean girl role.

"She called me a few times after high school," Toni said. "But we never met up. I felt a little guilty about it. She'd seen photos from our various reunions on Facebook, and she asked me why she wasn't invited." Toni's shoulders slumped. "I never knew what to tell her. Why do you ask?"

"Her name is Carla?" I asked to make certain. Olive could only remember that her mystery visitor's name started with a C. Nate was sitting on a stool at the kitchen counter. He looked curious and intrigued. I hadn't mentioned Olive's visitor because I knew it would worry him, and he might say something to Olive. I'd already stepped on her toes with my admonishment. The visit had seemed harmless, and the woman's excuse to be on the island for photographs was plausible. I'd almost let the whole thing go until Frannie's mention of a fifth woman came back to me.

"Yes, Carla Overton," Toni said. "That's her name now."

Betsy looked puzzled. "Why are you bringing up Carla?"

"I'm just trying to get a wider picture of your friend group." I wasn't ready to share any theories or let them know there was a chance Carla was on the island. It was still a farfetched theory too. The name starting with a C might have been a coincidence. "What can you tell me about her?" I directed my question to Toni because she seemed to have been the last person to talk to Carla.

"Carla?" Toni took a sip of coffee. "I think she divorced a few years ago, and she started a photography studio." Bingo. I was trying to keep a poker face, but Nate was picking up on the cues that I'd stumbled onto something. "I saw her mention it on Facebook. I was glad to hear that she'd moved on after the accident."

I practically slipped forward off the chair. Nate was catching on now too, but he had no idea that our suspect was on the island. "The accident?" I asked.

Toni looked toward Betsy as if to get permission to talk about it. Betsy took over. "In our senior year, the five of us decided to go skiing. I borrowed my uncle's big van, and we piled our gear into the back and headed up to the local resort. I hadn't wanted to bring Carla along. She wasn't very good on skis, but she made cookies for the trip, so we found space for her in the van. The roads were slippery on the way to the resort. I lost control on one curve, and the van slid off the road. Thankfully, a large granite boulder stopped us from sliding down the hill. The side of the van where Carla sat was crushed and her leg with it. The rest of us were fine, but Carla had to miss the last half of senior year."

"She went through three surgeries, poor thing." The reminiscing was making Toni feel even more guilty about the way they'd treated Carla. But had it been bad enough to push Carla to murder? Why else would she be on the island? And on top of that, she was left out of another reunion.

"How is her leg now?" I asked.

"The last picture I saw of her she was using a cane." Betsy squinted her eyes in suspicion. "What are you getting at? Do you think Carla followed us to the island?" She looked at Toni. "I told Rachel not to post about it on social media. Now we're being stalked by that loner? Just like she did in high school, always lurking around, listening in on our conversations. She's always been weird. I wouldn't put it past her to do something like this." Betsy was ready to run with it. "I'm leaving this island the second that ferry starts up."

"But Betsy, we have to stay and talk to the police first," Toni said. "We've got to do that for our friends."

"But what if crazy Carla is lurking around out there waiting to kill us next?" Betsy asked.

"We don't have any proof she's on the island," Nate said calmly. Boy, did I have something to tell Nate. "And I think it would be a mistake to leave before the police have a chance to talk to you. Otherwise, it might look like you're fleeing for another reason."

Betsy wriggled on her bottom. "What could be a better reason to flee than trying to keep away from a murderer?"

Toni looked at me with a weary frown. "She has a point. It's not safe here."

"No, it's not, but Nate is right. You need to stay until the police arrive," I said. "That is why you need to book rooms at the hotel. With this weather they are sure to have a lot of vacancies."

Toni nodded along as I spoke. "That's what I suggested yesterday. I'm going to call the hotel right now and reserve our rooms."

"Better yet, you're mostly packed. Get your things and Nate and I will walk you to the hotel. You can get rooms at the front desk."

"Should we stay together in a suite?" Toni asked Betsy. "Safety in numbers."

Betsy rolled her eyes. "I think that ship has sailed. We're safer in our own rooms."

Toni was hurt by the implication, but I had to agree with Betsy. If either of the two women were the killer, then they were safer alone behind a locked door.

I stood up. "Then it's settled. The two of you will wait at the hotel until the police arrive. I'm sure it won't be much longer."

Nate and I were already bundled up, and the heated house was getting warm. We stepped outside to wait for them.

Nate glanced back to make sure the door was shut and no one had followed us out. His mouth tilted in a grin. "Why do I get the feeling you know something that you haven't shared with your subordinate."

I grinned at him as I pulled on my gloves. "I spoke to Olive this morning, and she had a visitor last night." I checked the door too. We were still alone. "Olive saw a woman walking around on the trail near her house. She said she was out taking pictures and she got lost. Naturally, being Olive, she invited the woman in. Her name started with a C. That was all Olive could remember. But here's the kicker—she was using a cane to get around."

The weight of what I was saying struck home. His expression grew grim. "Is Olive all right? She invited a killer into her house. We need to make sure she doesn't do that again."

I patted his chest. "And that might be why I didn't tell you any of this earlier. I've already spoken to Olive about it, and she didn't take it too well. But if it is Carla Overton, then it's not such a stretch to think that Rachel opened the door for her. She wasn't a stranger, and maybe she felt sorry for Carla. It would explain why Carla's cane prints were outside the house."

The door opened and the two women came out. They looked anxious to leave the place, and I couldn't blame them. We dropped the subject for now. Nate hurried over to take each of their bags, and we started on our walk to the hotel.

eighteen

THE TWO REMAINING weekend visitors were safely checked into the hotel. A fierce wind, the last breaths of the storm, had kicked up again. Frannie hadn't been given clearance to cross the harbor yet. That meant Norwich wasn't even on his way, and now the murders were stacking up. It couldn't have been a worse weekend for a murder spree. (Not that there was ever a good weekend for one, but this weekend was particularly bad.)

I set out a lunch of leftovers—twice-baked potatoes, minestrone soup and chili—but everyone sat at the table staring glumly at their plates and stirring their food around as if that would help it disappear.

Nate was the only one with an appetite, but then, he was perpetually hungry. Opal also seemed more inclined to eat, but Tobias and Cora were wearing those same bored faces Cora and I used to wear at the end of summer when it was too hot to go outside and there was nothing fun left to do even if we did go out.

"All right, you two, we've been stuck inside a lot longer during big snowstorms," I said as I ladled myself a bowl of chili. This morning's adventure had given me an appetite like Nate's.

Tobias smiled weakly. "I'm sorry I'm not eating much, Anna. I'm so used to those morning swims that my body isn't sure what to do with all the stored energy."

"And since I'm not walking back and forth to work and skittering around serving tea, the last thing I need is a high-calorie feast like this." Cora reached for the last piece of bundt cake.

Opal watched her with an amused twinkle in her eye. "Yes, thank goodness there are low-calorie offerings like bundt cake on the table. Whenever I start a diet, I always make sure to start it off with a nice, fat slice of cake."

Cora shrugged with indifference and stared at Opal as she pushed a piece of cake into her mouth.

Opal rolled her eyes.

Tobias set down his fork and added more salt to his plate. "How is the murder investigation going?"

"Yeah, I could have sworn I heard the two of you walk inside saying something about a murderer hiding on the island," Cora said. "Just what this island needs—a resident serial killer."

Opal smiled wryly at me. I knew she was dying to bring up the island curse but then thought better of it. She returned to her baked potato.

"Is that true?" Tobais asked. "Sounds terrible. Was there another victim?"

"I was planning on talking about this after the food was cleared." I glanced at the corkboards. I needed to add another card and suspect, one that I was sure was our killer. "A second woman is dead at the Meyer house."

"Oh my," Tobias said. "I'm Jane and Harvey's accountant. That nice little beach house brings in a lot of money. This will not look good on their reviews."

Cora covered her mouth to avoid spitting cake out with her laugh. "Gee, do you think? *Great place to stay, wonderful view of the beach but watch out you don't get murdered.*"

We all laughed for a few seconds.

"Nate thought it being connected to a murder might increase its popularity," I said.

Nate had been fully absorbed with his lunch. He only looked up as I mentioned his theory. Everyone at the table looked his direction.

"Well, that was when only one woman was dead," he said.

I laughed. "So, one brutal murder is intriguing, inviting even, but two is where tourists draw the line?"

Nate nodded through everyone's laughter. "Yeah, yeah, now that you say it like that, this probably won't help their rental business."

"Especially if you don't catch the killer," Opal said. "Then everyone's business will be hurt, and our summer tourist season will be a disaster."

I wiped my mouth. "Let's hope we catch the person by then."

"Do you have a suspect in mind?" Tobias asked.

I got up and went to my desk to pick up the index cards and pen. "Actually, I don't need a new index card." Everyone watched as I walked over to the corkboards and unpinned the white index card with the question mark. I wrote down Carla Overton and held it up to explain.

"Carla was the obligatory fifth wheel of the group. According to Betsy, the proverbial high school mean girl, they didn't really like Carla, but she followed the group around. She did, however, get invited on an ill-fated ski trip. The van Betsy was driving skidded off the road, and while the others came out unscathed, Carla's leg was crushed. She went through several operations and missed out on the last half of senior year."

"Ouch," Opal said. "On two accounts. One for the multiple surgeries and the other on missing out on all the fun senior events—the prom, dances, graduation night. Everyone goes to school for twelve years just so they can blow off all their steam on a wild grad night. Do you think this woman, Carla, is on the island?"

"Yes, I'm almost positive. Not that we have anything to connect her to the killings yet aside from her footprints near the house."

"Well, that sounds pretty conclusive." Tobias salted his chili. He was eating more now that we'd taken his mind off his boredom.

"Footprints in snow aren't going to hold up in a court case, even with photographic evidence," Nate said. "We need a forensic analysis at the scene, but our hands are tied without law enforcement."

I frowned his direction. It took him a second to notice. "Oops, I said something wrong. I'll keep eating." Nate picked up his fork and plowed another bite of food into his mouth.

"It's not that you said anything wrong. It's that I've solved a lot of these without the help of forensics, and I plan to do it again."

"This woman is dangerous," Tobias said. "If she already killed two people—what's to stop her from continuing?" He looked at Nate. "I'm glad you're working on this with her."

It was time to frown at Tobias. He noticed and did exactly the same thing as Nate and picked up his fork. "Hmm, such a good lunch."

I laughed. "If I'm being honest, I'm glad to have Nate with me on this case."

Right then, Nate's phone rang. He pulled it out. "It's the other boss." He winked at me. "The construction boss." Nate stood up from the table to take the call. "Yeah, this is Nate."

He returned a few minutes later. "The site manager got us jobs cleaning up the island. Same hourly rate. I'm going to head out after I finish eating. Guess that investigation will have to wait."

"I've got a few things I need to do that I can do on my own... safely," I added before I got a round of disapproving looks. "I'll see you when you're finished."

Nate looked less enthusiastic about the island cleanup.

"Go. Frostfall needs some tidying up. I'll be fine. This isn't my first murder, after all."

nineteen

TOBIAS WAS BORED ENOUGH to volunteer to clean up after lunch. Cora and Opal helped. Everyone knew I was stressed about the murders. The weather outside could best be described as brittle and harsh. The sun was shining, but nothing about the day was inviting. The snow had an icy sheen and icicles dripped off the bare trees and house eaves. The remnants of the storm, namely the brutally cold and sometimes powerful winds, were still plaguing the island and leaving the harbor a frenzied mess.

I'd walked the two women into the hotel to make sure they had rooms available. Toni had pulled out her fancy gold-trimmed credit card and booked two suites. I'd made note of the room numbers because I wanted to talk to Toni alone, without Betsy. Betsy tended to take over the conversation, not to mention her penchant for getting defensive and suspicious. Toni was much calmer and easier to talk to.

The hotel lobby was nearly empty, but the hotel restaurant was busy. I pretended to read the menu, even though I knew it well. It gave me a chance to glance around the dining room for a customer with a cane leaning against a seat or table. I didn't see one, but I did see Betsy sitting alone at a table. She was eating a salad with one hand and scrolling through her phone with the other. I put down the menu and walked out before she saw me. I was sure if she knew I was talking to Toni, she'd want to be involved. I had friends like Betsy in high school; one, in particular, who always wanted to control everything.

I took the elevator up to the floor where Toni was staying, walked to the door and knocked.

"Who is it?" Toni asked.

"It's me, Toni. Anna St. James."

The door opened. I stepped inside, and she locked it behind me. "I thought that was you, but the peephole doesn't give a clear view. I worried it might be—you know—Carla. Do you really think she's on the island? I can't believe she'd do this. Carla wasn't so bad really. She was funny, and she was always easygoing and polite."

The hotel suites were nicely decorated with a coastal theme. Michael and I splurged on one when we first moved to the island and the house was being repainted. There was a living room, small kitchenette, bedroom and a bathroom with a jacuzzi tub. "Please sit," Toni said. "I'll make some coffee."

"Thanks." I sat on the sofa. The suite had an unobstructed view of the harbor. On a summer day, you'd be able to see the sun shining off the rippling water, sailboats floating gracefully across the surface and sea birds diving into the waves looking for lunch. Today, the harbor looked like a choppy basin of mud. Tree limbs and trash that had been picked up by the wind now floated on the turbulent surface. It was easy to see why Frannie hadn't gotten clearance yet. The harbor would need at least one more day to recover.

Toni came into the living room with two cups of coffee. "There's creamer in the refrigerator," she said.

"Black is fine."

Toni sat across from me on a chair. "It seems to me that ferry won't be moving today." She took a sip of coffee.

"I think you're right. It's too risky. Frannie, the ferry boat captain, is a good friend of mine. She is always very cautious."

"Good for her. She's got her passengers' lives in her hands, so I don't blame her."

"I saw Betsy just now in the restaurant. You didn't join her for lunch?"

Toni sighed. "It's too difficult to act chummy. First of all, neither of us were that close in high school. You might have gleaned that from our last conversation. I was closest with Ariel. Rachel and Betsy were close, but Ariel and Rachel were what you could call best friends. You know the politics and dynamics of a multi-girl friendship in high school. Loyalties get tested all the time." Toni shook her head. "No wonder so many of us need therapists once we become adults."

"You're right about that. My friends and I would be cozy and laughing and hanging out one minute, and the next, there'd be warring factions. You said Carla was always polite and kind."

Toni nodded as she took another sip of coffee. "Betsy ran things. Rachel helped us meet boys. Ariel was Rachel's sidekick, not quite as popular but well-liked and smart. Great in math."

I nodded. "It always helps to have a math person in the group. And you?"

"As Besty so harshly pointed out—I was the girl with the big house and endless allowance for trips to the mall and movie tickets. I wasn't naive. I wasn't as pretty or sporty or part of the cheer squad. I knew why they invited me into their circle of friends. But I didn't mind. You know how it is in high school. You work hard to fit in somewhere. Those friendships are what make or break your high school years." Toni's mouth turned down. "I do think we should be notifying the next of kin."

"I agree. This is such a tough situation. I have a friend at the mainland precinct. I'll call her and see what can be done. I've never had to deal with a murder when the island's been cut off from the mainland."

Toni's brows lifted. "You've dealt with murders before?"

"It's a long story, but as you've noticed we don't have our own law enforcement. And to be honest, the detective in charge of the island hates coming here, and he does a terrible job."

"So, you take over," Toni said.

"That's right."

An urgent knock on the door caused both of us to startle.

"Toni, it's me. Open up. I've got some big, terrible news." It was Betsy. She didn't sound upset, just anxious.

"Well, I'm alive and Betsy is too... clearly," Toni said as she walked to the door. "Who else is dead now?"

"Please, no more bodies," I said.

Toni opened the door. For a change, Betsy looked pleased so see me. Although there was a momentary pause as she tried to figure out why I was talking to Toni alone. Fortunately, her news had her too preoccupied. She held her phone and rudely shoved it into my face. "She's here. It says so on her website. No one else thought to look," she said snidely. "Carla is on the island."

I pulled back from the phone that she was holding too close to my face. There was a blog post on Carla's photography website. It said she was heading to Frostfall Island, a quaint island in the Atlantic, to take photos.

"You see. She's here and she's not taking photos. She's killing all of us," Betsy said. Her histrionics weren't making any of this easier, and it was upsetting Toni. "Toni and I need to get off this island." She turned to Toni. "Doesn't your dad have his own plane or helicopter, something that can pick us up from this horrid place?"

Toni smiled patiently. "There are no runways for a plane. It's all right, Betsy. We're safe here in the hotel until the police arrive."

"What a nightmare," Betsy muttered as she headed to the door and walked out.

Toni winced. "She's a little high-strung about all this. Betsy was always big on drama."

"I'm going to look for Carla. And you were right. You're safe here. I wouldn't venture past the lobby for now."

Toni walked me to the door. "Be careful. Obviously, Carla is not the kind and polite girl we knew in high school. By the way, how did Ariel die? You never said."

"We don't have anything definite until the coroner arrives, but it looks like a bullet." As I said it, we both came to the same conclusion.

"That means Carla's armed," Toni said.

"It sure looks that way. Thanks for the coffee. And try not to worry. You're safe in the hotel, and the police will be here tomorrow morning. I'm sure of it. I'll call my friend at the precinct on my way home. She'll put an extra bug in the captain's ear about the very volatile situation on Frostfall."

"Thank you. Stay safe," Toni said.

"You, too."

twenty

IT WAS cold enough outside that I decided to stay in the hotel and call my friend, Mindy. She used to live on Frostfall but now lived on the mainland. She worked at the precinct that covered Frostfall Island and where Detective Buckston Norwich had his office. I was sure he was sitting inside it right now, slopping mustard from a sandwich on his tie and alternately chewing on his toothpick (a habit that was as gross as it sounded). According to Mindy, Norwich rarely left his office. He preferred to work from his desk, which made him, possibly, the world's worst detective. Being called out of his cushy office to take the ferry across to Frostfall made him angry. He always arrived in a foul mood and ready to close the case fast, as an accident or by arresting the wrong suspect.

Mindy answered on one ring. "Anna? What's going on? Two murders in two days? That's a record even for Frostfall. Are you all right?"

"I'm fine but yes, we're not having a great weekend. First the storm and then a grisly murder, followed quickly by another. And according to my investigation, the killer is armed and loose here on Frostfall." I hadn't meant to alarm Mindy, but as I narrated what was going on I realized it was pretty darn alarming. "I know the ferry still hasn't been cleared to leave the docks, but is there anything we can do to get Norwich out here? Can the Coast Guard get involved?"

"We tried them. They're tending to vessels that were damaged out at sea. That storm was brutal. Norwich is, of course, trying everything to delay going to the island. But I've got the ear of the captain. I brought him some homemade brownies, so he won't mind if I give the whole thing a nudge. It's getting late now though, and the sun will be setting soon. It probably won't be until tomorrow morning. Are things secure for now?" she asked.

"Secure? Not sure that's the case when there's a killer on the loose, but there are two possible future victims. They've booked rooms in the hotel, and I told them not to leave. Hopefully, we've at least put an end to the murders."

"Oh, there's the captain now. I'll follow him into his office and let him know things are dire there."

"Tell him we need to contact next of kin, and I can send you numbers and names if needed."

"Right. They usually wait for the coroner or an official to confirm the deaths—"

"Oh, they're both dead. Believe me. See what you can do. And thanks, Mindy."

"You bet, Anna. And be careful."

"I will." I hung up and headed across the wharf. A bright red knit scarf caught my attention. Frannie was at the dock sweeping debris off the *Salty Bottom* deck.

"Hey, Fran," I called.

She looked up from her task. "Anna, come aboard." She opened the gate to her gangplank, and I stepped onto the boat. Frannie took good care of her ferry, but today there was a layer of mud and debris on the deck. "Can you believe this mess? I just called Joe to get down here and help. We're hoping to be up and running in the morning. I know you're anxious for me to pick up Norwich." She laughed. "Gee, never thought I'd use those words in one sentence." Norwich's reputation as a terrible detective was widespread. No one on the island respected him, and from what I'd heard, mostly through Mindy, no one in the precinct did either.

"I do need him here. There've now been two murders," I said quietly, even though we were very much alone out on the choppy harbor. The tide was still rough enough that I had to hold the railing to keep from falling over. Frannie, on the other hand, was a true sailor. She never had a problem with the motion.

"Two? In the same group of women?" Frannie set her broom aside and sat on a bench. "Sit before you fall over."

"Good idea." Sitting made me feel more secure, but there was still the matter of the motion and my stomach. I'd have to make our visit short. I didn't have time for a bout of seasickness. "I have something to show you." Now that I'd seen Carla's website it was easy to pull up on my phone. There was a nice photo of her standing in front of a giant redwood on the homepage of the site. I showed Frannie. "The other morning, you mentioned a fifth woman came to the island on a separate ferry. You thought she might be part of the reunion group. Is this her?"

Frannie took the phone and held it up to get a better look. "Well, she was layered in winter gear, but that looks like her."

"Did you happen to notice if she was using a cane?"

"Yes, now that you mention it, she was. She had some camera equipment or something, so I had to help her carry it off the boat."

"Did she happen to tell you where she was heading?"

Frannie pursed her mouth in thought. "Gosh, that was kind of a hectic morning, what with the warning messages from the Coast Guard and all, but there weren't many arrivals that day. She asked which direction to turn for Island Drive. Maybe she's in one of the rental cabins near Calico Peak. There's a lot of scenery up there for pictures." Frannie looked across the harbor. "Although nothing is very scenic after that storm. In fact, I mentioned to her we were probably going to get hit by bad weather. She said storm photos were her specialty. Why are you asking about her? Does she have something to do with the other women?"

"Yes, she's connected with them." It was best not to elaborate. I didn't need rumors swirling around the island until I was sure I had the right person.

"I knew it. She just had the same look about her. Funny though, she didn't mention anything about the reunion." Frannie stretched up to look past me. "Isn't that Nathaniel? He's with the cleanup crew, eh?"

I looked over my shoulder. Nate and a couple of men were gathering up fallen debris near the boardwalk. "Since they missed a few work days, the construction crew is out cleaning up the island."

"I, for one, will be happy when this island and harbor get back to normal," Frannie said.

"I'm with you. And now I will leave this rocking boat before you have more mess to clean up."

"Barf bags are in the wheelhouse," she said with a wink.

"And I'm hoping to avoid looking into one of those bags. Off I go. I'll see you later. Text when you get the O.K. to head over to the mainland. I'm anxious for Norwich to get here, and at the same time, I have to prepare myself mentally and physically for his arrival."

Frannie laughed as I left the boat. My feet and legs and stomach were very happy to get to solid ground. I hurried across the boardwalk. Nate spotted me and walked over to greet me. He glanced back. Some of his coworkers looked up to see where he was heading.

Nate waved his hand their direction. "Don't you have twigs to collect?"

They laughed and got back to work. Nate leaned forward and gave me a quick kiss.

"How is the investigation going?" he asked. "You're not doing anything dangerous, right? Tobias will never speak to me again if something happens to you."

"So only Toby will be upset if I end up on the killer's list?"

"No, I'd be sorry too." He kissed me again. "I'd be really sad not to have these lips to kiss. What are you up to, and don't tell me you're trying to track down the woman on your own. She obviously has a gun."

"Yes, I realize that. I talked to Toni. I also got confirmation from Frannie that Carla Overton arrived on the island just an hour after the other four women. And since no boats have left the island—"

"She's still here," Nate finished for me.

"Exactly."

"And now you're heading home so you can wait for me to help," he said with a wishful smile.

There was still an hour of daylight left. "I might go see Sera first just in case there's something they forgot."

Nate raised a brow. "Anna, it's not safe at that Meyer house."

"I know. I'll be careful."

"You leaving all this for us, Maddon?" one of the men called.

Nate rolled his eyes. "Coming." He snagged one more kiss. "See you later."

twenty-one

SERA and Samuel seemed to be tucked cozily inside their house. The wavering glow inside and the smoke curling up from the chimney told me to leave them be. Besides, I'd only used Sera as an excuse to walk this direction so Nate wouldn't worry. Although, Nate knew me well, so he probably saw right through that excuse.

The Meyer rental, Frostfall's new horror house, looked quiet and inviting under its white cloak of snow. The gray-blue shingles had shaken off most of the snow and ice, and there was just enough snow piled on the multipaned windows to give the house a holiday card look.

The front path had been trampled on so much that the snow had melted and turned to a slick layer of ice. I was no longer wearing the unwieldy spikes on my boots, so I walked carefully next to the path as it was far easier to traverse crunchy snow. Toni and Betsy were both so anxious to pack up and leave the house that I hadn't noticed anyone taking the time to lock up. Poor Jane and Harvey had no idea what was happening at their pristine, charming beach house. What a mess it would be for them.

I reached the front door, and out of habit and caution, I knocked. As expected, there was no answer. I realized I was holding my breath as my gloved fingers turned the knob. I stepped inside. The stylish décor and cozy interior didn't help the silent, grim ambience in the house. I wondered if our killer had already discovered that her last two potential victims were gone. I hoped that was the case because it meant she wouldn't be returning.

I had no idea what I was looking for, so I wandered around. The light outside was fading fast. I wouldn't stay long. I never minded walking around the island in the dark, but it was different when there was a killer wandering around with a gun.

Betsy and Toni had cleaned up the house, most likely to make sure they got their cleaning deposit back. Considering the horrific mess in the bedroom, it seemed like a waste of time.

Once Norwich arrived, I needed to have evidence to prove I'd found the killer, otherwise he'd take off on his own unsubstantiated tangent and arrest the first person who crossed his path. Nate and I had been to the house enough, he might even try to pin it on one of us. Samuel had been the first on the scene after Rachel's death, so there was nothing to stop Norwich from arresting him.

I walked to the kitchen and pulled out the trash can. I'd found that trash was a good place to start in an evidence search. The trash was stuffed with empty wine bottles, food scraps and not much more.

I looked down the hallway. I'd already seen more than I wanted of the murder scene. As Nate said, it was now up to forensics to find evidence in that room. I glanced in the bathroom. It was clean too. A small trash can sat on the floor near the vanity. Not wanting to push my hand into the mounds of tissue, I shook the contents around. A flash of pink caught my eye. I reached in gently and pulled the tissue out. It was smeared with the same pink that was on the wall. Had Carla taken the time to use the bathroom and wipe lipstick off her hands after brutally murdering Rachel? It seemed odd. Maybe Rachel had left pink on the tissue when she wiped off her makeup the night she was killed. I left the pink tissue on the vanity. So far, my efforts to find evidence, other than the murder weapon, had been futile.

It occurred to me then that there was a second murder scene. Nate and I had been so shocked by the second body that we never searched the shed for evidence. I stepped out the back door. The path that Betsy had shoveled was clear and dry from the day of sunshine. I walked toward the shed and opened the door. We were already going to hear a lecture about moving Rachel's body, so we'd left Ariel untouched on the ground.

The interior walls of the shed were lined with beach chairs, an umbrella, a kayak and some rafts, all things for summer renters. Rachel's body was on a work table that took up most of the center of the shed. There were a few tools and gardening supplies piled in a corner. I concluded that Samuel and Nate moved those things off the table to make room for the body. Ariel's paper flowers were placed on the table next to Rachel. Late afternoon shadows were blotting out the dim light in the shed. I pulled out my phone, turned on the flashlight and crouched down next to Ariel. The blood on the back of her head had dried into a black matted mess. There were no other marks on her hands or the side of her face that was still visible. Since she was shot in the back of the head, she probably never saw it coming.

A soft sound behind me caused me to push to my feet, but I'd reacted too late. A sharp pain shot through my head, and all the light in the shed vanished. Darkness. I never saw it coming.

The pain was excruciating, like the world's worst headache. It didn't take me long to realize I hadn't just woken up in my cozy bed. The ground beneath me was hard and unforgiving, not soft and comforting like my mattress. The room was dark and cold and quiet. I touched the side of my head, the place where the pain was the worst. I winced and pulled my gloved fingers away from what seemed to be a sizable bump. I glanced around in the darkness. I wasn't alone. Then it all came back to me in a nightmarish wave. I wasn't alone at all, but my two companions were dead. I was in the shed behind the Meyer house. My heart beat faster as my eyes swept around the small space. The movement made my head throb more, but I had to be sure that no one else was standing in the shed.

More of the terrible moment was coming back to me. I'd crouched down near Ariel's body, and I heard a noise behind me. I stood up, but before I could turn toward the noise, something hard hit my head and I blacked out.

A flash of light caught my eye. It was my phone. The flashlight was still on, but it had fallen beneath the table in the center of the shed. I crawled on hands and knees to retrieve it. It was past five. I'd been out for a good twenty minutes. There was no one around to ask me questions to check my brain status, so I asked myself a few.

"Name? Anna St. James."

"Where are you at right now? I'm sitting in the shed on the Meyer property, and the dead women are Rachel and Ariel." It was possible talking to myself while sitting in the dark was a significant sign that something was amiss, but then how else could I assure myself I was all right? My head certainly ached, but everything else seemed to be working.

"Name Santa's reindeer," I said, then paused. "Really? You couldn't just ask about the days of the week? Let's see—there's Comet and Cupid, Donner and Blitzen, Prancer and Dancer and Dasher and Vixen and, of course, Rudolph. Vixen? Is that right? Who on earth named that poor reindeer?" I pushed to my feet. The ground under me seemed to rock as if I was back on Frannie's boat, but a few seconds later, I felt like I was on solid ground. It seemed I'd passed my personally developed test for proper cognition. With any luck, I'd leave this horrifying situation with only a headache.

The door to the shed was shut. I walked to it and paused for a second. Would my assailant be waiting outside to finish the job? I couldn't stay in the shed any longer. It was cold, and I needed to get home. Everyone would be worried. I pushed on the door once and then harder. Someone had latched it from the outside.

I looked at my phone. Who would lecture me the least? I was about to see if Winston was in the area when I heard footsteps outside. I backed into a dark corner of the shed and turned off the light on my phone. The latch slid open briskly, and the door was yanked open.

"Anna?"

I nearly crumpled in relief. "Nate, I'm here." I stepped out from the corner.

"Jeez, Anna, I was so worried." He pulled me into his arms. I couldn't stop the tears.

I peered up at him. "Thank you for not lecturing me. I'm not really feeling up to it right now."

He hugged me again. "That's all right. I've got a whopper saved up for later. Let's get out of this shed, and you can tell me what happened."

"All right, I'll tell you, but you're not gonna like it. However, you'll be happy to know that I can name all of Santa's reindeer and all without Google assistance."

Nate looked at me with a worried brow as we stepped out of the shed.

I patted his arm. "Don't worry. It's all part of the story."

"You mean the one I'm not gonna like?" he said.

"Yup."

Nate pulled the shed door shut, and we walked toward the road.

twenty-two

MY WONDERFUL *FAMILY*, including my actual family, Cora, hovered over me with worry for a good hour after Nate and I returned home. Opal brought me refreshed ice packs every ten minutes, and Tobias insisted on sitting right next to me on the sofa. Every few minutes he would shine a penlight into my eyes to check the size of my pupils. Cora brought me hot tea. She was probably the least attentive of those around me, but I sensed she was worried. The bump on my head had gone down a lot since I initially felt it.

Nate stood by, watching over me as if he worried I'd take off and do something silly again. I told him the only thing that was silly about the whole affair was that I came out of the ordeal empty-handed.

Cora and Opal assigned themselves the duty of putting dinner on the table. It didn't require too much effort because I had plenty of food in the freezer to heat up for a nice winter supper. They chose the individual vegetable pot pies I'd made the weekend before. I wasn't in the mood to eat much. My head was starting to feel better, but the constant throbbing pain made me queasy. Cora and Opal had gone out of their way to set a nice table and light candles. Cora even made a chopped salad. It was probably only the third time I'd seen my older sister put on an apron and prepare food from scratch. I couldn't disappoint her by not eating it, so I sat at the table and nibbled as much as I could.

My fork was reluctantly going in for another round when I glanced up and found everyone was watching me with concern. "What? Did I grow those horns after all?" I reached up for the invisible horns and then remembered too late that there was a tender bump on my skull. I winced.

Opal sat up straight. "Should I get another ice pack? I've got one chilling in the freezer." She moved to get up.

"No more ice, Opal. It's like compounding a brain freeze on top of a migraine." Opal looked a little hurt by my comment. I was not back on my game yet. "Of course, ice was exactly what I needed to bring down the swelling," I added. That seemed to make her feel better.

"You're not eating as much as usual," Tobias noted. "That could be a sign of a concussion."

"While I love to have my extra big appetite pointed out to me," I said with a smile, "It's just the headache. It's like a migraine and those always make me queasy."

"So, you don't like my salad?" Cora asked. Her reputation for making everything about her remained untarnished, even if she had experienced a bout of worry.

"All right, everyone," Nate interrupted. "I think we should relax so Anna can relax."

I smiled at Nate and everyone reluctantly pulled their focus away from me and back to their plates.

"I really like the olives in the salad, Cora," Tobias said. Given Tobias's love of salt, it made sense he enjoyed the addition of briny olives to the salad. I personally thought they were out of place but would never, ever say anything.

"Thank you, Toby." Cora sat up primly and grinned as if she'd just created a culinary masterpiece. If I knew my sister, and I did, she'd be giving me pointers the next time I attempted a salad.

I pushed aside an olive, certain my stomach wanted nothing to do with it, then something struck me. "Olive," I blurted.

Cora rolled her eyes. "Oh, for goodness sakes, if you don't like them, just push them aside like I'm doing with the annoying peas in the pot pie." She pointed at her impressive pile of peas.

"Not this olive." I looked at Nate. "We need to warn her. I mean I did warn her once, but she didn't know that the lost photographer was dangerous." I wiped my mouth. "I need to go see her."

"Surely not," Tobias said sternly. "You can't possibly go out there in your state and at night." He looked at Nate for backup.

Nate knew me well enough to know I was going no matter what.

Nate sighed. "I'll walk with you."

Cora and Opal tried to talk me out of going, but I insisted it would be a short visit and with Nate by my side, it would be fine. I packed up a few goodies for Olive. I never liked to show up empty-handed. We pulled on our winter layers and headed out.

The cold air ended up refreshing me, and by the time we got moving on the trail, my head felt better than it had all night.

"I think all I needed was to get out and move," I said.

Nate smiled over at me. "You can say that all you want, but I assure you Toby will be waking you every two hours tonight in case you have a concussion. He told me his plan earlier, and I told him I'd help by taking a few shifts."

"You guys really don't have to do that."

"You were out for a stretch of time. Santa's reindeer or not, you probably have a concussion. I love living on this island, but there's something to say for living in a city where an urgent care and emergency room are just minutes away."

I couldn't argue with that. We reached Olive's house, and I sighed audibly with relief when I saw smoke rising from her chimney and a light on in her kitchen. We could hear her talking to Johnny and the bird responding with some song lyrics as we knocked on the door.

A few seconds later, Olive opened the door a crack and peered out. "Anna, Nate, it's you." She pulled open the door. Warm air rushed out. "I wasn't sure who it was. It certainly has been a day of visitors."

We stepped inside. "What do you mean?" I blurted once the door was shut. "What visitors?"

Olive lowered her face coyly. "I know you warned me not to let strangers into the house, but since I'd already met Carla once before, she wasn't really a stranger."

Nate rested a hand on my shoulder to silently calm me down. I took a steadying breath. "Carla came back here?" I tried to sound normal, so as not to alarm her, but it wasn't easy. I'd had a tough day, and I was tired and there was nothing I wanted more than to be in my bed. The whole case was really getting to me.

"Yes, she dropped by with a bottle of wine as a thank you gift." Olive pointed the bottle out. It was on her coffee table along with two glasses. "I couldn't very well turn her away when she'd brought a gift. We sipped wine and talked for several hours. She's very polite and funny and extremely talented. She showed me some of her prize-winning photos on her phone. I showed her my art studio, and we even sat down there and painted for an hour. She loved Johnny, and he was his usual entertaining self. All in all, it was a lovely visit, so you see, nothing to fret about."

"I wish that were the case," I started, then the ache in my head reminded me of something. "Wait, what time did you say Carla was here?"

"Let me see. That's right. I'd just had my afternoon tea when she knocked at the door. That would have been half past two. She left just as the sun set, possibly five. Why do you ask? Are you still worried she has something to do with that murder? I'd find that surprising given her pleasant disposition."

I looked at Nate. "That would have been the time you got

—" Nate started but stopped before spelling it out. Olive didn't need to know about my attack.

"Got what?" she asked.

"That's about the time I got back home," I said quickly. "Did Carla happen to mention where she was staying on Island Drive?"

"We didn't discuss that, but she mentioned she had a stunning view of the Old Man of the North Lighthouse from the back door of her rental."

"That must be the Graystone cabin. It's the only one with that view," I said. "Well, Olive, we're sorry to have bothered you, but here's a few goodies for the rest of the weekend."

"You sure do spoil me, Anna." Olive took the basket into the kitchen. She pulled out the cookies and vegetable pot pie and handed me back the basket.

Nate and I said goodbye and stepped out into the cold night air. The island already looked much better after the cleanup.

"Carla couldn't have been the person to attack you in the shed," Nate said.

"Not unless she could be in two places at once. We need to talk to Carla, but not tonight. We'll go see her in the morning and find out exactly what is going on. The only thing calling me right now is my warm, comfy bed."

twenty-three

I WOKE to the smell of burning toast. The sun was muted by clouds, but the light still hurt my eyes. I sat up slowly, stiffly. My head, neck and shoulders still ached from the attack. I glanced at my phone. Frannie sent a text a few minutes earlier that she was on her way across the harbor and that she'd return with Norwich. It didn't happen often, but I was relieved to know the detective was on his way.

Someone knocked tentatively on the door. I knew who it belonged to. Tobias had followed through on his plan to wake me every two hours. Twice, it was Nate's groggy face at the door.

"I'm getting up, Toby," I called. "All is well." I glanced at the clock. It was after eight, at least three hours later than my usual rise time. Sleeping this late was going to make me drowsy and off my game for the rest of the day.

"I'm glad to hear it," Tobias said through the door. "Opal and Cora are downstairs making breakfast."

"Yes, I sensed that." I'd made cinnamon rolls for Sunday breakfast, but they were still in the freezer. I'd been thrown off schedule by the knock on the head.

Tobias chuckled as he walked away.

I walked downstairs. Nate tried to hide a smile behind his coffee cup. It seemed scrambled eggs and toast were on the menu, only the kitchen looked as if a feast for a hundred people was being prepared.

"Don't worry. We'll clean this up," Cora said before I could wipe away the look of shock.

Winston had returned home. Obviously, Cora and Opal had filled him in on everything. He gave me the same look of concern as everyone else. "How are you feeling, Anna?" he asked.

"I'm fine. Just a little soreness in my neck. How are the animals? How is Alyssa?"

Secretive looks were exchanged, and smiles were being tamped down. Cora had an especially bright twinkle in her eye as she smiled at Winston. "Go on, tell her," Cora coaxed.

Winston blushed and shrugged. "I asked Alyssa to marry me, and she said yes."

"Oh Winston, that's wonderful." He stood up for my hug.

"My timing isn't great. I'd been planning this proposal for months and then I saw the storm forecast. But it turned out all right. I popped the question in candlelight and in front of a roaring fire."

"Sounds incredibly romantic," Cora gushed. She had those stars in her eyes she always got whenever the subject of engagements and weddings came up.

"I'm so happy for both of you," I said, and I really was, only enthusiasm and glee weren't in my arsenal this morning.

"I heard about the murders." Winston motioned toward the corkboards. I hadn't even kept up with the case. I had so much more to add, but I didn't want to miss our chance to talk to Carla.

"Don't worry about that. We'll get it sorted. Be sure to tell Alyssa congratulations for me." I sat down and Opal set a plate of eggs and charred toast in front of me. She looked quite proud of the breakfast she'd prepared. "Thank you, Opal. It looks delicious."

"Liar," she said wryly. "But eat it anyway. You look pale."

"I feel pale." I smiled up at her. "Is that a thing?"

"It sure is," Cora sat with her plate. "I've felt pale many times, especially when I haven't eaten enough or I've had too much wine."

"I think that's lightheadedness," Tobias said as he showered his eggs with salt. I watched him destroy the food I cooked every day, but Opal acted as if it was the first time he'd used salt on his food.

She put her hands on her hips. "I salted the eggs plenty."

Tobias felt chastised and put down the salt shaker.

Nate set down his cup of coffee. "Hey, Winston, the animal rescue is off Island Drive near Calico Peak. Did you happen to notice if the Graystone cabin was occupied this weekend?"

"Actually, yes, we noticed the chimney smoke and lights on in the evening. I thought it was odd that someone rented the place at this time of year, especially on a stormy weekend."

"Well, you know as well as anyone that you can't time things around a storm," I reminded him. I yawned. I'd fallen asleep fast but being woken every two hours had given me some quiet reflection time in the middle of the night. It was highly likely that Carla was not the killer. Hopefully, we'd find out more about her visit to the island when Nate and I walked to the Graystone cabin.

"I suppose we should hurry over to that side of the island so we can talk to her," Nate said.

"Talk to who?" Cora asked.

"Our possible suspect," I said. Nate was right. The ferry was up and running. That meant all three women would be leaving the island soon, and I was sure one of them was the killer. Was it possible my attack was unrelated to the murders? It didn't seem likely, but if it was the case, then Carla would still be at the top of the list. And then there was brusque, unlikable Betsy. She was very quick to discover that Carla was on the island. Just like she was quick to pin the whole thing on her. Toni was quiet, appearing the most innocent of the three, but sometimes that was all a ruse.

Opal joined everyone with her plate. It was funny to see her on the other side of the table doing the serving instead of waiting to be served. "Have you figured out who hit you on the head? Is it the same person who killed the two women? Is Norwich on his way?"

"Norwich is on his way, and at the moment, I have no idea who hit me or who killed the two women." The topic of murder wasn't sitting well with me this morning. I changed it to a much more delightful one. "Winston, I know the engagement is brand new, but have you two decided on a time and place? You can have a ceremony here at the house if you like."

Cora practically leapt off her seat. "Oh my gosh, yes, please. I can help plan it. I have some experience with weddings."

Opal laughed. "*Some* experience. Most people don't have a couple hundred thousand to throw away on a wedding."

Winston smiled and nodded. "Opal's right, Cora. We don't have the budget for a big wedding or a small one. We'll probably just take a trip and elope. But we would love to have a party here at the house afterward."

"Wonderful." I picked up my cup of coffee. "Cora, you can help plan that. But no ice sculptures or live swans or cheesecakes flown in from Tuscany. We'll keep it simple."

"Perfect," Winston said.

Opal sighed. "We're sure going to miss you and your sweet little menagerie, Winston."

"I'll still be on the island, and if Alyssa and I get overwhelmed with rescues, I'd still love to count on you guys to feed and take care of the occasional gull or pelican."

"Absolutely," I said. I lifted my cup of coffee. "Here's to Winston and Alyssa. Two wonderful souls who deserve nothing but the best."

Everyone raised their cups. It seemed I was going to have to find a new boarder soon. But for now, I needed to find a killer.

twenty-four

EVEN WITH THE BURNT TOAST, I discovered I was hungry enough to eat all my breakfast. I downed two cups of strong coffee and two aspirin, which made me feel better. I felt almost myself again as Nate and I headed out on a brisk walk to the Graystone cabin. We decided to take the west side of Island Drive because the cleanup crew had shoveled away most of the snow, and it would be easier.

As we passed the harbor, I glanced at the docks. Frannie hadn't returned yet. Sometimes she had to wait for Norwich and his team. She hated that, but there was nothing she could do. We needed officials on the island, and they worked on their own schedules, not ours.

The red roof of the Frostfall Hotel glistened in the sporadic splashes of sun. Clouds had moved in overnight, but they were wispy and moving across the sky fast. Shadows came and went quickly. At the moment, the sun was in full view.

"You know, let's pop into the hotel for a second," I said. "I want to remind Betsy and Toni that they need to stay on the island until Norwich talks to them. Betsy was particularly anxious to leave."

We crossed the wharf to the hotel. The restaurant was slow for a Sunday morning. I glanced inside the dining area but didn't see either woman. Frannie would have told me if they'd been on the first ferry out, so I could only assume they were still in their rooms.

We took the elevator up to the suites. I wasn't entirely sure why, considering Betsy's unlikable disposition, but I knocked on her door instead of Toni's. Betsy yanked the door right open. She was wearing a green sweater, leggings and slippers.

"Did you find her?" she asked before I could say hello. "Did you find crazy Carla?"

"Not yet." I glanced past her into the room and noticed her snow boots were sitting next to the sofa. "Did you go out yesterday afternoon?" I asked.

She looked taken aback by the question. "With Carla, the homicidal maniac, still on the loose? No way."

Just then, the door to Toni's suite opened. "I thought I heard your voices out here. What's happened? Have the police arrived?"

"They're on their way," I said. Toni was last on my suspect list, but I still needed to ask. "Toni, did you leave the hotel yesterday afternoon?"

"Gosh, no. Like you said, we're safer in the hotel."

"But I knocked on your door at three to borrow some

hand lotion." Betsy showed her hands. "Look how rough and red mine are in this harsh weather. Can't wait to get back to Texas."

I had little patience today. "You were mentioning about knocking on Toni's door."

"Right and she didn't answer. Which reminds me, Toni, can I borrow some hand lotion?" Betsy was particularly annoying this morning.

I looked at Toni. "Did you leave?"

"No, I was here in the hotel. Down in the restaurant."

It was a plausible answer.

"We'll leave you for now," I said. "Detective Norwich will be in contact soon."

"Tell him to find Carla so we can finish this nightmare and go home." Betsy shut her door sharply.

Toni turned on an apologetic smile. "Sorry she's so rude." Toni was always the picture of polite serenity. "I hope we'll be able to help the detective some, but as you know, neither of us have much to tell. He'll finally be contacting families, right?"

Toni had asked about next of kin being notified several times, but Betsy never brought it up.

"Yes, he'll be taking care of that, and the coroner's team will be with him. I'm sure the Coast Guard will assist with getting the bodies back to the mainland, and from there, the families can plan arrangements back home."

Toni looked tired and close to tears. "Those poor families. My poor friends. This is all so awful. It's still hard to believe this has happened."

"It's been a terrible weekend on the island," I said. "I'm sure we'll see you later."

"Take care and stay safe," she said.

Nate and I got on the elevator. I looked over at him. "Well, my silent partner, how did I do?"

"Couldn't have done better myself. But I would have asked Toni what she ate. Tried to throw her off in case she was making it up. Three o'clock is an odd time for a meal."

"Well darn, I hadn't thought of that. Guess I still have a lot to learn. I'm thrown off by Toni's calm countenance. Nothing about her says killer. Whereas Betsy is as volatile as a stick of dynamite in a burning shed." The door to the elevator opened.

We walked through the lobby, but I took a sharp turn toward the restaurant. The Sunday morning hostess was a young woman named Jill. She was straightening a stack of menus at the hostess podium.

"Anna, are you here for breakfast?" She smiled sweetly at Nate and picked up two menus.

"Not staying for breakfast. I was wondering—who was working as hostess yesterday afternoon at three?"

"I'd have to look at the schedule, but I'm pretty sure it was Arlene."

"That's what I thought. I'll have to come back later to see her."

Jill put the menus back on the pile, looked around and leaned forward. "Is this about the murders?"

I was stunned speechless for a second. "How did you hear about them?"

"There's a woman staying in the hotel. Tall, athletic type with a loud voice. She was up at the front desk telling Megan that two of her friends were murdered, and a fifth friend from high school was somewhere on the island waiting to take her out too. Megan told Randy and Randy told me. It all sounded very scary." Jill couldn't have been out of high school for more than five years. "I still remember my friends and me in high school. Every day was a new soap opera, if you know what I mean. Not that any of us would have resorted to murder. Although my friend, Penny, did key Veronica's car when she caught her kissing her boyfriend." She rolled in her lips. "Sorry, I'm sure you don't have time to hear all this, what with two murders on the island." Her mouth turned down. "Does that mean that sloppy detective is coming to the island? Sometimes he stops in here to eat. He always leaves his spitty toothpicks on the table, and he rarely tips."

"Yep, that sounds like our sloppy detective. He should be here soon. Oh, and Jill, I'd appreciate it if you didn't mention the murders to anyone."

"Sure thing, Anna, although news travels fast with this staff."

"I understand. We'll see you later."

Nate and I walked out of the lobby into the brisk air. "Did I make up for my earlier mistake?" I asked. "I just have to come back and talk to Arlene and see if she remembers seeing Toni."

"Yep, good save." Nate took a beanie from his pocket and pulled it down low on his head. "Guess I'll be back on that scaffolding tomorrow. Seems like the storm is finally gone."

"We're back to regular winter weather, which for Frostfall, means a lot of warm layers, especially if you're out on scaffolding. By the way, something interesting happened back in the hotel that I haven't mentioned yet." I peered over at him to see if he had any clue what I was talking about.

"Uh, let me see," he said. "The snow boots sitting by the sofa in Betsy's room?"

"Seeing those was what reminded me to ask her if she'd gone out. It seemed funny that those boots were out but not so farfetched as to put her in the murderer hotseat. This doesn't have to do with boots. Yesterday, I went to the hotel, and I knocked on Toni's door. She asked who it was before opening the door. You know how the peepholes give you a distorted view of the person outside. Toni told me she worried it might be Carla. At that time, we were all pretty convinced that Carla's arrival on the island was not just to take photos. It was too big of a coincidence. I was sure Carla was the killer, and I think Toni was too. That was why she opened the door cautiously."

"Whereas, Betsy opened it fast, too fast to even check the peephole," Nate said. "As if she didn't have a care in the world."

"And certainly not as if a killer might be standing on the other side," I added.

"Well done. It's those little things that can be easily overlooked. Either Betsy is just impulsive and careless, or she didn't worry about meeting up with the murderer because she already knows who did it."

"Exactly. Betsy said she didn't leave the hotel yesterday afternoon, but it's possible she's lying."

"Gee, do suspects lie?" he asked facetiously.

"All right, Mr. Detective, that probably went without saying. Let's see what our most recent number one suspect has to say. Somewhere along the way, someone has got to crack."

twenty-five

THE GRAYSTONE CABIN was owned by David Graystone, a widower who only came to the island with his grandchildren for two weeks each summer. His wife, Marilyn, died some years back. The cabin was her favorite place in the world, so he never had the heart to sell it. The cabin's wood siding had been weathered to a salty gray, and the windows badly needed a coat of paint. I'd only been inside the cabin once, when David decided to have a summer party. The décor wasn't charming and welcoming like in the Meyer house. The furniture was functional and practical for a year-round rental. It wasn't as popular as the Meyer house (at least pre-murder) but the view of the Old Man of the North Lighthouse kept it a sought-after property.

We stopped at the paved walkway that led up to the front door. "How are you feeling?" Nate asked. "Are you ready for this?"

"Sadly, no. The headache is mostly gone, but I'd be lying if

I said the attack didn't leave me feeling less than enthusiastic about this case. I'll be just as glad to hand it off to Norwich today."

"Now I know you're not feeling yourself." Nate leaned over and kissed my forehead. "Even with a concussion and lack of sleep from two annoying pests waking you up every two hours, you'll still do a better job than Norwich."

I reached up and pushed a strand of hair off his face. "Having you by my side this weekend makes it all much more bearable."

"If only I'd been at your side the *whole* weekend," he said.

"You're not taking blame for the bump on my head. That was all my doing." The path hadn't been cleared. I could see the print from Carla's cane in the slushy snow. A light was on inside, but there was no smoke coming from the chimney. It made sense if she was planning to leave the island this morning.

I knocked on the door. A small, paneled window allowed me to see inside the cabin. There was a suitcase sitting in the entryway. A cane was leaning against it. A woman with brown curly hair and wearing a bulky sweater the same brown color as her hair came around the corner with a profound limp.

She hesitated a moment, then smiled and opened the door. "Mr. Graystone didn't mention he had more renters coming to the island this morning. I'll be out in a few hours. I'm just waiting for the next ferry." Carla had kind brown eyes. She didn't look as fashionable and put together as the other women. She had that sort of artsy, carefree look about her, just like my dear friend, Olive.

"Actually, we're not tenants," I said. "You're Carla Overton?"

"Yes, that's me." Her brow wrinkled in confusion. "I'm sorry, do I know you?" After Olive's high praise, I expected her to be more friendly. It was time to namedrop.

"I'm Anna St. James and this is Nathaniel. We're good friends of Olive Everhart, the painter who lives in the sweet cottage overlooking the beach."

Her smile widened. "Yes, Olive is wonderful. I spent some time with her yesterday. Her parrot is such a character. Almost makes me want to go out and adopt a bird."

"Johnny is amazing," I said. "We also know a few other friends of yours."

Her mouth pulled down at the corners. She nodded. "Come inside. It's freezing out on that stoop."

We followed her inside. Her right leg was constantly struggling to keep up with her left.

"Does it pain you a lot?" I asked.

"More so in the winter." She led us into the small front room. The drapes were open, so we could see the tower on the lighthouse. The sky was a gorgeous winter blue, and the sun reflected off an ocean that had calmed down considerably since the storm.

Carla pointed to the chairs, and she sat on the small sofa.

"How did you hear about my leg?" she asked.

"I'll explain a little about myself first. Frostfall Island counts on the mainland police to handle crimes on the island. I step in sometimes in the interim while we wait for law enforcement." It was always hard to explain my unorthodox role as island investigator. Carla nodded along, but she still looked confused.

"I see," she said. She clearly didn't. She looked at Nate. "Are you law enforcement?"

"I'm her occasional partner," he said. "I'm not with law enforcement." The last words seemed to stick in his throat.

I was done with my prologue. Time to get down to business. I cleared my throat to get her attention back on me. "I learned about your leg from Betsy and Toni. They told me about the accident on the way to the ski resort. I'm sorry that you've had such a struggle with it. I'm sure it hasn't been easy."

Carla glanced down at her right leg. "I've adapted and it hasn't stopped me from an adventurous life behind the camera."

"Yes, Olive told me you were a talented photographer."

"That was kind of her."

"Carla, I know you came here to take photos of Frostfall, but it was very coincidental that four of your friends from high school also came to the island for a reunion. It's especially so because of the terrible weather."

"Well, storm photos are my specialty. You know—Mother Nature at her wildest and rawest. It makes for the most stunning photographs. I can show you a few." She moved to get up from the sofa.

"I'm sure they're beautiful, but for now, let's focus on your friends. You weren't invited along for the reunion, and yet here you are."

Carla straightened her bulky sweater and sat up straighter. It seemed she was ready to put up a defense but then slumped down again. "All right, confession time."

Both Nate and I inched forward with interest.

"Rachel and Ariel were posting about the reunion on Facebook. I knew I wasn't going to be invited. I was kind of the *other* friend in that group. Occasionally, they'd invite me along or let me sit with them at lunch, but I was never part of their close circle. I would be lying if I said I wasn't hurt when they didn't invite me to their reunions. I'd never heard of Frostfall Island until they posted photos of the island and the cute house they'd rented. I did some research and I thought it looked like a beautiful place to take photos. The storm was just an added bonus. I found this cabin on the rental site and booked it for the same weekend. But I haven't had contact with any of them. I went to the wharf to take photos, and some of the locals were talking about two murders at the Meyer house. I saw Toni and Betsy walking to the hotel, so it was easy for me to figure out that Rachel and Ariel were the victims."

"But you went to the house Thursday, the day or night before Rachel was murdered."

Carla looked surprised. "How did you know?"

"Your cane leaves a distinctive print in the snow," I explained.

Carla looked over at her cane. "I guess that makes sense. I did go to the house. It was just after dusk before the storm really got going. I'd been out at the swimming beach for a few hours taking photos, and I knew their rental house was close by, so I walked there." She chuckled sadly. "I talked myself into believing that they'd be glad to see me. I imagined being invited in for a glass of wine and chat. But I never went up to the door. My pride wouldn't let me knock. 'Carla,' I told myself, 'if they wanted to see you, they'd have invited you.' The wind was getting worse and the snow was falling faster, so I headed back to the cabin. Like I said, I never had contact with them."

Her explanation was plausible and disappointing. The unusual footprints had been a key piece of evidence.

"Let me ask you, Carla, is there anything from the past that might have caused one of the friends to turn on the other?"

"Oh, I don't know—it was typical high school stuff. Sometimes they were best friends, and other times they were angry with each other. I was always on the outside edge, so I guess I had a better view of the drama than the people in the middle of it. Rachel did steal Ariel's boyfriend, Clark, which caused a temporary rupture in the friendship, but Ariel took up with another boy. Betsy was the catalyst for the whole thing. She was mad at Ariel, so she started a rumor about Ariel cheating on Clark. He turned just as quickly to Rachel."

"Why was Betsy mad at Ariel?" It still seemed ridiculous to be chasing down a decades-old motive, but I wasn't sure which direction to go.

"Ariel was always mad at Betsy for one thing or another. Betsy could be abrasive. I think Ariel wanted to borrow some history notes or something, but Betsy wouldn't give them to her. So, when Betsy snuck into the girls' restroom to smoke a cigarette, Ariel informed the hall proctor. Betsy got suspended and lost her softball scholarship. Her parents couldn't afford to send her, so she had to stay home and go to community college."

"Seems like that would sting for a while," I said. I was acting as if wasn't a big deal, but I was sure I'd just stumbled onto a motive for killing Ariel. But why Rachel?

"They were friends again by the time graduation rolled around." Carla perked up suddenly. "I can't believe I forgot this. Now that you brought up Thursday night—I decided to turn back down the road and head home." She waved her hand at her leg. "My gait is slow, and the weather made it even slower. I heard a noise behind me. I glanced over my shoulder and noticed a tall figure. I couldn't see more than that in the dark, but it looked like a man, big shoulders and build and he was at least six feet tall. I'm not entirely sure where he came from, but he was looking at the beach house. To be honest, it freaked me out enough that I hurried my pace. I never looked back." She pressed her hand to her chest. "My cowardice might have cost Rachel and Ariel their lives."

"It's hard to know that for sure, but this is good information," I said.

"This has been so upsetting. I'm anxious to get off the island. Do you know if the ferry is running yet? I need to get back home. A friend is watching my cats, and they'll be missing me."

"The ferry is running, but I suggest waiting for a later

one. Once the detective arrives, I'll be letting him know the details of the case," I said it with a straight face as if Norwich would be interested in my information. "I'll have to mention that you're here since you know both victims. He'll want to ask you some questions. It sounds like you have some significant information to tell him."

Carla sighed. "I suppose that shouldn't take too long."

Nate and I stood up. "Thank you for speaking with us."

"I'm sorry I couldn't be more help," she said as she walked us to the door.

We said goodbye and walked back toward Island Drive. "At first it sounded like you found motive," Nate said. "But that last minute piece of information throws a whole new twist into this."

"It sure does. Maybe our killer is a tall, broad-shouldered mystery suspect. But what motives did he have to kill those two women? Or is there a homicidal maniac on the island? I guess we'll have to leave that to the real detective." My phone beeped and I pulled it out of my pocket. "Aha, I thought I smelled something unpleasant in the air. Norwich has landed."

twenty-six

NATE and I waited outside the Meyer house for Detective Norwich. If we met him at the dock, he'd probably send us both on our way before we even handed out one detail. I usually left out most of the things I'd uncovered. Granted, it was the competitive side of me that liked to hold back. But he was the professional, and it didn't seem right that he counted on me to give him free information. If he did his job right, which was rare, then he'd uncover the same things I'd uncovered. Since the talk with Carla, I was leaning heavily toward Betsy as an important suspect. She had motive. It'd been more than twenty years since Betsy was caught smoking in the girls' room, and the two women had seemingly made up after the incident, but losing a valuable scholarship affected more than just your high school years. That big mistake would have followed Betsy right into adulthood. She wasn't able to go to the school of her choice or continue with her softball career. Her future dreams ended when she got caught and suspended, and from what Carla said, Ariel caused the dominoes to fall by telling on her friend.

"I just realized I'm hungry," Nate said. The two of us were shuffling around a lot to keep warm.

"Seems like the words 'I'm hungry' are a vital part of your vocabulary. I'm feeling much better now, so I'll whip us up some lunch after we talk to Norwich. Correction—after *I* talk to Norwich. As much as he hates me, he despises you."

"Guess I'll stay quiet like I did in Carla's house."

"Yes, just like that." I glanced over at him and laughed. "You're like the ultimate fashion accessory: attractive, eye-catching but not too flashy."

Nate nodded. "Yep, I can live with that. And here comes Mr. Wonderful right now." We both turned to look down the street. Norwich had his oversized trench coat belted around his big waist. He was talking animatedly to the officer who was stuck as his partner today. It was a young male officer who looked as if he'd rather be working with anyone else but Norwich. I figured there was always a tense moment amongst the uniformed officers as they waited to see who was going to be unlucky enough to be assigned to accompany Norwich to the island.

I took a deep breath. "I can't believe I was anxious for him to get here. Now all I can think of is how nice it'll be to see him step on the ferry and float away."

"St. James," Norwich said with a nasal tone. "And you, Maddon," he sneered and lifted his upper lip. "I figured I'd see the two of you waiting here." He sneered again at Nate. "Two murders in one weekend. Great work, Maddon."

Nate raised an angry brow at him. "Uh, I believe I should be saying that to you, since this island is in your jurisdiction. You see, I'm just a resident."

I leaned closer to Nate. "Pretty accessory, remember," I muttered.

Nate sealed his mouth shut and nodded once.

"As you heard, there are two victims." I put on my professional, talk-to-the-investment-broker tone. I hoped I could get out all the pertinent information, avoid his usual barrage of insults and call it a day. "Four women arrived on the island Thursday morning. They rented Jane and Harvey Meyer's beach house for the weekend. Rachel Bingston was murdered in her bed sometime late Thursday night or early Friday morning. The second victim, Ariel Frasier, was murdered Saturday morning."

Norwich's mouth pulled into his infamous smirk. "You certainly like to throw the 'M' word around a lot." He glanced behind him. The county coroner and his assistants had just reached the road. "The coroner and I will determine whether or not it was murder."

I rolled my eyes. "Right. We'll let you decide." I led him to the door. Normally, by now, he would have sent me on my way, but he knew he was already two bodies deep and way behind on the investigation.

I waved my hand. "Down the hallway to the last door."

Norwich and his apologetic-looking assistant passed me and headed down the hallway.

Nate leaned closer and lowered his voice. "If he figures a way to label either death an accident, I will eat my gloves."

"St. James!" Norwich bellowed. "Where is the body?"

I heard Nate sigh loudly as he followed behind me. The room had a stale blood smell. I rubbed my nose. "I left word at the precinct that we'd moved the body to cold storage, a shed at the back of the property. Given the way it smells with just the bloodstains, I'd say that was a good call."

Nate was tired of being a pretty accessory. "I asked a neighbor to help me move the body. We took photos of the crime scene before we moved the victim. We didn't touch anything else in the room. Ms. St. James found the possible murder weapon in the shrub outside the window." Nate waved toward the knife.

Norwich's lip twitched. He yanked out the toothpick he'd been chewing. His face scrunched in agitation. "It's more than obvious what happened here," he said, almost nervously. His assistant seemed to be coming to the same conclusion, the same one Samuel and the women had come to. "This was the work of the serial killer." The officer gasped and nodded in agreement.

"It's not PTK," Nate said.

Norwich scoffed. "What would you know? You're just a civilian," he said snidely.

The coroner and his team reached the room. "Oh my," he said as he looked around.

Norwich pulled out his phone. "I'm going to call it in. We need Detective Maxwell and Roberts to come investigate. They're on the PTK case."

"Roberts and Maxwell will tell you the same thing I'm telling you. And they'll be much less gracious about it," Nate said. "You'll be wasting their time. And the second victim was shot in the back of the head."

Norwich paused before dialing. "Where is the second victim? Don't tell me you moved her, too? You don't remember anything about police procedure, do you?"

"We didn't need to move her," I said sharply. "She was shot in the storage shed as she placed paper flowers around her dead friend. No lipstick. No pillowcase. No knives. This was clearly a copycat murder. The second one wasn't as elaborate, just boom and the victim was dead. You're wasting time calling the other detectives. You need to get moving on this case before the three possible suspects leave the island. Two are in the hotel and the other is in a cabin on Island Drive. The woman on Island Drive might have seen the killer." I was talking fast because I was losing him. "Are you even interested in names?" I asked. My voice was getting higher, and I felt my frustration level reach its peak even earlier than usual with Norwich.

Norwich laughed. "What are you saying, St. James? That you know the name of the PTK? Or maybe it's someone you know well." He shot a suspicious squint at Nate. "Always thought it was a little strange how you gave up on finding the killer."

I felt Nate tense next to me. I took his arm. "Let's go. Obviously, he's got it all in hand." I had to practically drag Nate down the hallway.

We stepped out into the cold air. Some of the tension melted from Nate's posture.

I looked up at him. "He's an idiot and we know it. Let him

call Maxwell and Roberts. They'll let him have it when they realize they came to the island for nothing. And the bonus is you'll get to see a couple of old friends." The last part seemed to placate him more, so I tossed in the final words that I knew would make him happy after our unpleasant encounter with Norwich. "Grilled cheese and tomato soup?" I asked.

It took a second, but a weak smile finally broke. "Still the best partner I've ever had."

twenty-seven

WITH THE WEATHER greatly improved and the island cleaned up enough for easier travel, my housebound family had splintered off in various directions. Tobias decided to head to his office and finish some work so he'd be caught up when he opened in the morning. Cora was bored enough that she texted Sera to see if there was some work to do in the shop before tomorrow's reopening. Sera was more than happy to have her help. Opal had a Judy Garland marathon lined up on her DVR, and Winston was back at the refuge, no doubt making wonderful future plans with Alyssa.

Nate and I sat down to gooey grilled cheese sandwiches and hot tomato soup. "I put three kinds of cheese on the sandwich because you looked like you needed three kinds."

Nate pulled apart the sandwich halves. The mozzarella did its usual stubborn act of staying attached to both sides. A long white strand of cheese dangled for a few seconds before Nate opened his mouth wide and snatched it from midair.

"Hmm," he moaned as he finished the bite. "You're right. This is definitely a three-cheese day." He shook his head. "This island and, most especially, you, are a good influence on me. A year ago, if Norwich had spoken to me like that, the man would be picking up his teeth right now. There was a time when my temper could get the best of me, but this new life— it puts everything in better perspective." He reached over and touched my cheek. "You put things in better perspective." Nate picked up the sandwich. "And your grilled cheese sandwiches don't hurt either." His phone rang as he took another bite.

He wiped his hands on the napkin, chewed down the bite and pulled out the phone. "It's Jake—Detective Maxwell," he clarified before answering. "Hey, Jake, what's up?" Nate put the phone on speaker and placed it on the table. He knew I was interested in what was going on.

"Roberts and I got a call from Norwich. He said the PTK is on Frostfall Island, so we're at the dock waiting for the ferry. Given Norwich's track record, I thought I'd call you to see what was going on. Do you know anything about it?"

"I do. I'm sitting with Anna right now."

"Anna, the woman who solves murders on the island and who also has stolen your heart?" Maxwell chuckled into the phone.

"Yes, that Anna, and now I regret putting you on speakerphone."

"I'm on speaker? Anna, whenever Nate meets up with us for beers, you're all he can talk about." There was a muffled sound. "Hey, Roberts, we're finally going to get to meet

Anna." Maxwell returned his attention to the call. "Roberts is at the fried shrimp stand buying lunch. I told him to leave me off his shrimp feast. I get seasick just thinking about that ferry ride. Maybe I should be talking to Anna," he said.

"Hello, Detective Maxwell," I said toward the phone. "I think for this particular case Nate is better informed."

"Is it our killer?" Maxwell's tone was more serious now.

"No, it's a copycat," Nate said. "They used a serrated blade, like a bread knife. The writing, the message, the color of lipstick were all wrong."

"Great, so I'm going to have to go through a bout of seasickness just to let that imbecile Norwich know that he is yet again dead wrong."

"I don't know what to say, buddy. My word is no longer official. I do look forward to you telling the imbecile he's dead wrong, though. It took all my self-control and my beautiful Anna to keep me from throwing my fist at his smirking face this morning."

"Sure wish we didn't have to follow through on this. Your word that it's not PTK is all I need, but like you said—it's not an official call." He chuckled. "And yet, there is no one I'd trust more to make that call than you."

Nate stared down at his plate of food. Maxwell's words had touched him.

"Thanks, Jake. But I'm not part of that world or that investigation anymore." His voice was slightly hoarse. "Come here, check it out for yourself. I'm sure you'll reach the same conclusions. I guess we'll see you soon."

"Since we're making the trip," Maxwell said, "any chance

we can sample some of those delicious homemade baked goods you're always bragging about?"

Nate lifted his eyes my direction.

I leaned toward the phone. "I think we can make that happen, Detective Maxwell."

"Please, call me Jake. Now that blasted boat trip doesn't sound so terrible."

"Wha's goin' on?" Roberts asked over a mouthful of food.

"Jeez, Roberts, get that smelly, greasy shrimp away from me. I'm already going to be hugging the railing on that boat as it is. I don't need that smell in my nostrils. Maddon says it's not the PTK."

"What? Then why are we making this trip? My kids wanted to go to the movies this afternoon. They were mad I couldn't take them." Food crunching came through the phone.

"You're an animal," Maxwell said. "Who shovels three shrimp in at once?"

"Sure you don't want some?" Roberts asked.

"I'd rather poke my eyes out with my own fingers. Besides I'm saving room for some of Anna's baked goods." The two men were having their own conversation as if we weren't also on the call.

"No way," Roberts said. "Do you think she'll make those brownies Maddon is always bragging about?"

I raised a brow at Nate. He was in the middle of what I called a Nate blush—no color change, but his dark lashes dropped and a crooked smile turned up his mouth on the right side. Nate shook his head. "Hey, Abbott and Costello, you're still on the call."

"I'll make brownies," I said.

"Woohoo," Roberts said.

"We'll see you guys soon. Anna and I will walk down to meet the ferry. And Maxwell, stay close to that railing."

Nate hung up the phone and put it in his pocket.

"I'll let Frannie know to text when she's close to shore, so we can head down there." I got up to carry my dishes to the sink. "And now I guess I better pull on an apron and make brownies."

"Sorry about that. I guess I've been doing a little bragging lately about my wonderful girlfriend and her many talents."

"I don't mind." I filled my sink with warm water for the dishes and couldn't stop the smile from bursting free.

twenty-eight

FRANNIE WAS HOLDING back a laugh as Detective Maxwell lumbered quickly off the boat. He was a big, burly guy with red hair and, at that moment, a greenish complexion. Detective Roberts was smaller in stature. He had a sort of gruff Paul Newman look about him with a piercing blue gaze and dashing smile.

There were a few man hugs, not really embraces but a lot of loud claps on backs and shoulders. Nate looked positively thrilled to see them, and he seemed equally pleased to introduce me. "Jake Maxwell, Owen Roberts, this is Anna St. James." Nate's grin widened as he looked at me.

"So pleased to meet both of you," I said. I shook Roberts' hand, but Maxwell insisted on a hug.

With greetings over, we headed in the direction of the Meyer house. "I'll let Anna give you a rundown of what's happened here so you can quickly assess the scene, toss the required insults at Norwich and head back to Anna's for brownies."

Maxwell hadn't recovered yet, but Roberts was more than anxious for the brownie portion of the visit. I briefly filled them in and then Maxwell and I fell into step a few paces back from Roberts and Nate.

I looked up at Maxwell. "Was it very bad?" I asked. The harbor had looked relatively calm considering the chaos the storm had created.

Maxwell patted his belly. It wasn't round, but it wasn't flat. It looked as if the man enjoyed his beer. "I'll be ready for those brownies in a bit, but for now, I'm just glad to be on solid ground."

"I'm the same way," I said. "I was sitting on the boat with Frannie, the ferry captain, and the boat was docked, but I still couldn't wait to leave the deck." I didn't add in that the tide was wild because of the incoming storm. My words seemed to make him feel better.

"I don't know why, but I've always had a problem with motion sickness," Maxwell said. "When I was twelve, I was at friend's birthday party. His dad videotaped it and then we sat down to watch a replay of the party. Well, his dad wasn't exactly Martin Scorsese. The video jumped from room to room with no transitions, and the video cameras were as big as our boomboxes back then, so it was hard to hold steady. It was like sitting in the back of a wild roller coaster ride but without the track ahead to tell you which way you were heading. I got sick right there in front of all my friends."

Roberts and Nate were just ahead of us talking about mountain bikes. Roberts looked back. "Have you ever heard of that? Someone getting motion sickness while sitting on a living room floor." He laughed loudly. "Of course, he told me that story one night when he'd had too many beers, so I made sure everyone in the precinct knew about his harrowing experience watching a birthday party home movie."

Both men stopped to take in the ocean view as we passed the wharf. "So, this is why you're hiding out on this island," Roberts said. "And, of course, there's Anna." His smile definitely had shades of Paul Newman.

Maxwell took a deep breath. "That fresh air helps. Gotta admit, it wouldn't be too shabby waking up to these views every morning."

The conversation was so enjoyable, it was easy to forget that we were heading to a double murder scene and Detective Norwich.

Norwich must have seen us coming up the road. He stepped out onto the front stoop with his hands stuffed importantly in his pockets. His belly hung out over his feet as he tried to puff out his chest. His rooster stance deflated some when he noticed Nate and me tagging along.

"We don't need any civilians at the scene." Spittle flew past the toothpick as Norwich spoke.

Maxwell, who stood a head taller and a half-person wider than Norwich, looked back at Nate and me. "They're with me," was all he said. "Now show me the crime scene."

Norwich sneered at the two of us, then turned to go inside. Maxwell and Roberts went in next. I noticed Samuel and Sera coming down the road. I'd had more than my share of Norwich and the Meyer house murders, so I walked out to see them. Nate stayed behind, anxious to watch Norwich's face fall to the floor when Roberts and Maxwell told him he was wrong.

"We saw you and Nate walking with two men," Samuel said. "It looked like Jake and Owen. We rode with them last time we were on the mainland."

"That's who it is. Norwich called them here because he insisted Rachel was murdered by the PTK."

"But Nate was sure it wasn't him." Samuel looked confused, and Sera looked frightened.

"It wasn't the serial killer, but Norwich wouldn't listen to Nate." Voices pulled our attention toward the Meyer house. The men were in the backyard now, heading to the shed.

"How are you feeling?" Sera asked. "Cora told me you took a blow to the head. Even if the PTK isn't here, it seems we have a vicious killer on the island."

"That reminds me, did the two of you see anyone, a tall person, specifically, hanging around the Meyer house? Not just Thursday but at any time this weekend?"

"The only tall person around my house is this guy." Sera tilted her head toward Samuel.

"We didn't see anyone," Samuel said. "Did one of the women remember a tall person hanging around? They never mentioned it the morning after the murder."

"This came from another witness, a fifth friend who came to the island under the guise of taking photos, but she was hoping to join the reunion. She came by Thursday night before the storm really took hold, but she never found the courage to join her friends. She said she saw a tall person standing near the house as she walked away."

Samuel's brows creased. "Well, if someone came down the road, the witness would have seen him walk past."

"Unless they cut through one of the yards," Sera said. "Otherwise, he's right. There's only one way to the end of this cul-de-sac."

"That makes perfect sense. But maybe you're right. Maybe they cut through someone's yard. It was so chaotic that night with the wind and thunder, I doubt anyone would have noticed or heard a stranger cutting through."

Animated voices pulled our attention back to the house. Nate came out first and then Maxwell and Roberts followed. Norwich stepped out on the stoop, his face purple with irritation.

"What a moron," Roberts said as they walked toward us. "Hey, Sam, I forgot you lived on this little chunk of land too." There were new greetings and introductions. Nate pulled me aside while his friends met Sera and talked to Samuel.

"How did it go?" I asked.

"As good as expected. Maxwell told Norwich he should have listened to me and saved everyone a lot of time. Officer Trenton, the one with Norwich, already did way more work than the detective, finding names and getting phone numbers. Norwich handed Trenton the duty of notifying kin. Roberts laid into Norwich for not handling it himself. Maxwell told Norwich to contact the other women, take statements and make sure they didn't leave the island yet.

Norwich just stood there, his face getting redder with each order."

"So, what about those brownies?" Maxwell bellowed. "My stomach is feeling better, and it's empty as a base drum."

"That's the sound I was hearing," Roberts quipped.

I smiled at Sera. "You two are welcome to come for some brownies."

Sera took Samuel's arm. "No, thanks. We've been working since six this morning. All I want to do now is take a hot bath and put up my feet. It was lovely meeting you both."

We parted there and the four of us headed back to the boarding house. I peeked over my shoulder at the Meyer house one last time. As usual, Norwich was sneering at me.

twenty-nine

MAXWELL AND ROBERTS were wonderfully entertaining. Cora and Opal had joined us for the brownies. Of course, both men, one divorced and the other a confirmed bachelor, were falling all over themselves to impress Cora. And, of course, my sister was delighted by all the attention. They were hesitant to leave, especially Maxwell, who was now going to board the ferry with a belly full of brownies. When Frannie texted to let me know she was about to take her last harbor crossing of the day, they pulled on their coats and said their goodbyes.

Nate came in the back door after walking them to the dock. Forlorn—that was the only word I could think of to describe his expression as he stepped inside. Seeing it pulled at my heartstrings. He released his frown temporarily to greet Huck, then it appeared again.

"Coffee?" I asked.

"Sure."

I always considered coffee the piping hot elixir that could cure the blues. It was a fantasy to think that a cup could help convince him that his life was better and more fulfilling on the island. Seeing his friends, especially acting in a professional capacity and with the PTK mixed in, had triggered some feelings of homesickness. I caught the same pensive expression while everyone talked and laughed and ate brownies. We caught each other's gazes more than once during his friends' visit, and without exchanging a word, I knew exactly what he was thinking.

I brewed the coffee. The sun was setting on the island, and the long winter shadows began to take shape outside. Nate was at the table picking at the few crumbs of brownies in the pan. I'd made two batches and sent each man home with a chunk.

I set a cup of coffee down in front of Nate and sat across from him.

"They absolutely adored you," Nate said. "As I knew they would."

"And Cora?" I asked.

Nate smiled faintly. "I think Roberts was ready to propose and that says a lot considering he's never married or even dated anyone longer than a year."

"He wouldn't be the first lifelong bachelor to be bitten by the Cora bug." We silently sipped our coffees until I worked up the courage to talk about the subject we were always tiptoeing around.

"You miss it terribly, don't you?" I asked.

Nate stared down at the cup nestled between his hands. "Sometimes. And other times I remind myself how stressful the job was. Seeing the worst side of humanity at every turn—it does something to a person's soul. As rewarding as it was to catch a killer, it never brought back the victim. There was still a tragedy tied to the success of finding the killer. But I do miss it occasionally, especially when I hang out with my ex-partners." Nate lifted his dark blue eyes to me. "But I have a new partner, and I'd miss her much more."

"I'd miss my partner, too," I said. It was time to drop the subject. Nate had to sort this out on his own. "Did Norwich leave the island on the last ferry?"

"He wasn't at the dock. Frannie mentioned that the Coast Guard was sending a boat to collect the bodies and take the coroner team back to the mainland. I'm sure Norwich will ride with them."

"Did you see any of the women?"

Nate shook his head. "Now that you mention it—no, they weren't leaving either. I wonder if Norwich was actually doing his job and interviewing them."

My phone rang jarring us out of our conversation. I walked to my desk and picked it up. "Hey, Sera." I immediately heard sniffles and short, clipped breathing. "Sera?" My tone caught Nate's attention. I shrugged.

"You've got to get down here right away, Anna," Sera sobbed. "That imbecile—" She took a deep, ragged breath. "That stupid detective is arresting Sam for murder."

"What? That can't be."

"Hurry, Anna, please. I don't know what to do."

"Nate and I are on our way."

Nate was pulling on his coat. "Another body?" he asked.

"No, Norwich is arresting Sam for the murders."

Nate's jaw clenched tight as he pulled on his coat. "I know I said earlier how you and the island have helped mediate my temper, but this guy is really standing on my last nerve right now. Whatever happens after this—I apologize in advance."

It was dark and there were plenty of slick, black ice spots on the trail, but Nate and I practically ran the entire way. We met Norwich with his suspect at the corner of Sera's road. Samuel's jaw was clenched as tightly as Nate's. His bare hands were bound. It was a cold night to be without gloves. Officer Trenton had a hard time looking anyone in the eye. He knew this was yet another reckless false arrest. Norwich was famous for them.

"Thank goodness, Anna, Nate," Samuel said. "Tell this detective that he is making a big mistake." Samuel glowered at Norwich. It was rare to see Sam angry. "And when I do call my lawyer, it'll be to sue you for false arrest."

Sera came running down to meet us. "Can you believe this?" She was holding a tissue, and her eyes were red and puffy.

"Don't worry, baby, I'll be back home soon. This guy has nothing to hold me on. I know who to call once I get to the station."

Sera reached for Samuel's arm, but Norwich put up his hand to stop her.

"At least let him put on his gloves," Sera said. "It's too cold for bare hands."

"Fine," Norwich said begrudgingly.

"The gloves are in the pocket of my coat." Samuel tilted his head to show which side.

Sera moved to get the gloves. Once again, Norwich put up his hand. "Not so fast. I'll get them." Norwich dug in the coat pocket and pulled out one glove and reached into the other pocket but came up empty handed. "Which hand do you want to keep warm?" He waved the single glove with a smug grin.

"I must have lost one. I had them shoved in the pockets the morning that I went to see why the women were screaming." He looked pointedly down at Norwich's potato-shaped face. "I rushed out of the house hoping I could help them," he added. "Never pulled the gloves on."

Norwich sneered. "Save it for the interrogation room." That comment made Sera sob into her tissue.

"On what grounds are you arresting this man?" Nate's official tone came out, but it was edged with plenty of emotion.

"Are you his lawyer?" Norwich asked.

Nate's fists were curled but still at his sides as he moved a little closer. "You have no evidence. You're doing your usual sloppy investigation, and you're looking for a quick, easy conclusion."

"For your information, an eyewitness saw a tall man outside the house where the woman was stabbed."

Nate looked at him in utter disbelief. "You're arresting him because he's tall? I know you're a terrible detective, but this is really bad even for you."

"Neighbors saw the suspect entering the house in question in the early hours of Friday morning." Norwich's jowls wobbled as he spoke.

"I told you I went over there because I heard a scream. The woman was already dead," Samuel said.

"Likely excuse," Norwich muttered.

"Yes, it is, because it's the truth," Samuel said.

"And then there's the dark hair we found on the first victim. It was short like the suspect's. Forensics is going to run DNA samples when we get him back to the precinct. I won't be surprised if it's a match."

"I won't be either," Samuel said. "Like I told you, I helped Nate move the body into the shed. My hair could have easily been on the victim."

"For that matter, it might be my hair," Nate said.

Norwich's lips pulled into an evil grin. "Then maybe I'll be back here tomorrow to take you away in handcuffs. Guess you shouldn't have moved the body."

Norwich knew he was outnumbered, and he was starting to fidget like a caged animal. "The Coast Guard is on its way. The coroner is already at the docks with the bodies, and we're riding back with them. Unless you want me to arrest every single one of you, I suggest you step out of the way."

Norwich wasn't going to back down, and I worried that Nate would throw a fist and end up getting arrested too.

"Samuel, don't fret," I said. "I'll get to the bottom of this. You'll be back on Frostfall soon." I looked at Norwich. His upper lip was twitching. "Once again, I have to do the job that you failed to do right. Prepare to be shown up and humiliated, yet again."

Norwich sneered at me. "Get out of the way before I put you in handcuffs."

I stared at him for as long as I could stomach, then stepped back.

Nate and I walked Sera home. I'd never seen her so upset. Nate started a fire for her, and I fixed her a cup of hot tea. "I'll get him back home, Sera. Don't worry."

"But how?" she asked.

"The three women, the most likely suspects, are still on the island. I'm going to talk to all of them again. Carla, the woman who claimed to see a tall man outside the house when she was leaving—something about that didn't seem right. She told me she heard someone behind her and looked back. She could only see a silhouette, so she was far away from the person. With the howling wind and loud thunder, I don't see how she could have heard anyone's footsteps."

"Especially in the newly fallen snow," Nate added.

"Exactly."

"But how will you keep them on the island?" Nate asked. "They'll be anxious to leave in the morning, and if Norwich hasn't asked them to stay—"

I pulled out my phone. "Fortunately, I'm good friends with the ferry captain." I dialed Fran. "Hey, it's me. Can you do me a favor? Can you pretend the ferry is having engine trouble in the morning?"

"I suppose so. Monday morning and winter weather means there'll be very few passengers. Are we keeping someone on or off the island?" she asked.

"We're keeping someone on. Three women, in fact. And my intuition tells me at least one of them is a killer."

thirty

NATE and I were energized and ready to tackle the case. Somehow, I'd convinced myself that Norwich would get the job done this time, and I'd have a break from my side job, one I never asked for. But now, more than ever, it was crucial for me to solve the case. Samuel and Sera's lives had been turned upside down in a matter of minutes by one wholly incompetent detective.

The second we got home, I grabbed a pen. I hadn't been keeping up with the board. Again, it was based on my delusional thinking that Norwich was going to handle this double murder on his own.

I took off my winter gear. Dinner would have to come from the freezer again tonight. Samuel's arrest took precedence. I picked up my pen and walked over to the corkboards. "Carla Overton admits to going to the house the night of the murder. She claims not to have gone inside, but I'm putting a question mark after that because suspects lie.

She claims to have heard someone behind her, a tall man with broad shoulders. He was at the opposite end of the road and yet she was able to hear his footsteps in soft snow during a loud storm. She has a solid alibi during the time of my attack." I looked at Nate. "Should I still count my attack in all this?"

"I'd say there's a substantial chance it's connected to the murders."

"Darn that bump on my head. It puts a wrench in my main theory that Carla came to the island to kill the friends who treated her so badly in high school. Which reminds me." I pulled her card free from the pushpin again. "Carla was the only person hurt in that accident. You'd think that would have garnered her nicer treatment from the other friends, especially Betsy, who was driving the van." I wrote down a few notes about the accident and how it caused permanent damage, enough that Carla had to walk with a cane.

"What about Toni?" Nate asked. "You never got a chance to check out her alibi about being in the restaurant when Betsy knocked on her door."

"That's right." I pulled Toni's card off the board. "I've been guilty of forming opinions about possible suspects based on their demeanor. Toni is much calmer and easier to talk to than Betsy, so I pushed her to the bottom of the list. But right now, everyone is on the list at the same position." I stuck her card back and slumped as some of my newfound determination slipped away. "What if it wasn't any of the women? What if there is some tall, broad-shouldered mystery suspect running around the island? Worse than that

—what if he already took a ferry to the mainland? He could be long gone, and Norwich will never find him. He'll just formally charge Samuel and—"

Nate walked over and put his arms around me. "Easy there, tiger. It'll be all right. Your first instincts are usually right, and you knew right off the bat that one of the friends was the killer." We cuddled for a moment. His soapy scent, warmth and strong arms were all I needed to regain that determination.

"We'll set out first thing in the morning to interview the women," I said.

This time it was his enthusiasm that took a hit. "You're on your own, boss. I got a text from the other boss that we're back on the jobsite tomorrow. That worries me. Whoever did this had no qualms about hitting you on the head. They could've killed you. In fact, they might have thought that was the case."

"I'll be fine." I pulled Betsy's card off the board and wrote about the 'smoking in the girls' room' incident that got her suspended. It was good reason to dislike Ariel, but why kill Rachel? And it was so long ago that it seemed like a stretch. Besides that, they'd obviously repaired their friendship after that. I added that Betsy had opened her hotel door freely without any concern that a killer could be standing on the other side. I pinned the card back on the board.

"I suppose I better figure out something easy for dinner. Everyone will be hungry and, murder or not, people need to eat. I've got some marinara in the freezer. I'll put it in the microwave to thaw. Then it's just a matter of cooking noodles and putting a few slices of garlic bread in the broiler. I think I'll call Sera after dinner to check on her. She was my rock after Michael disappeared. I need to show her that I'm her rock, too." My throat tightened at the thought of poor, wonderful Sam sitting in a jail cell or an interrogation room.

I pulled the sauce out of the freezer and put it in the microwave for a quick thaw. Nate was scrolling through his phone. "Let me know what I can do to help," he said. His face popped up. "This is interesting."

"Oh, please tell me you found a photo of the actual murder taking place, so we can wrap this up tonight. I hate thinking about Sam in jail."

"Sam's in jail?" Cora practically screeched as she stepped into the kitchen. "What happened?"

"Norwich." It was all I needed to say.

"Well, we have to get him out. What should we do? I have some jewelry I can pawn so we can post bail."

"That's nice of you, Cora, but the best thing we can do is find the real killer. What did you find, Nate? You said it was something interesting."

"I thought I'd look for the women on Facebook. It's been mentioned enough that I figured each of them were active on it." He stood up and walked over to me. "These are a few old posts from Toni."

I took the phone and scrolled through the posts. She was talking about the Pillow Talk Killer in most of them. Apparently, she was part of a group who'd taken it upon themselves to find the serial killer. She posted articles and grisly details and theories.

"Wow, she knows a lot about the killings," I said.

"Everything except the details that we keep from the public, like lipstick color and specific wording in messages."

A small detail came back to me. "There was a tissue in the bathroom trash. Someone had wiped the pink lipstick color off on it. I considered that it might have been Rachel removing her makeup before bed, only when you wipe off lipstick there's a significant amount left on the tissue. This was only a light smear."

"Could have been the killer trying to rid herself of damning evidence," Nate said. "You and I searched that property the morning Rachel was discovered. There were no footprints around the house or near that open window. I think it's safe to conclude the killer was either inside the house or was invited in through the front door."

I looked across to the corkboards. "Then the murderer is on one of those index cards, and tomorrow, I'm going to find out which one."

Nate rubbed his temple. "Maybe I should take the day off."

I'd had little enthusiasm for this case but with Samuel's arrest, I was fired up and ready to nail the murderer. "Nope, I've got this, partner."

thirty-one

I HAD no time to waste. Frannie was already doing me a huge favor by skipping the first run across the harbor. She'd texted me an hour after my request and told me that Joe wanted payment in the form of one of my famous German chocolate cakes.

Nate had eaten an early breakfast, bundled himself up and headed out to the lighthouse. Tobias came back from his first swim in days. He said he missed it so much; he wondered if he'd been a dolphin in an earlier life. The member of my crew who was already certain about her previous life took a breakfast sandwich to go. Not that she was going anywhere except upstairs to read one of the many novels she had stacked on her nightstand. Sera was still terribly distraught, but she decided to open the shop. It hadn't been open since Thursday, and she couldn't afford to keep it closed. Cora left early, knowing that Sera was going to need more help and support than usual. Nate had mentioned that living on the island had changed his way of looking at life. The same could be said for my sister, only she wasn't aware of it. Not long ago, the notion of leaving early to go to a job would have been inconceivable in her spoiled, trophy wife brain. But this morning, she'd come down ready to go so she could help ease some of Sera's burden.

With the breakfast hour taken care of, I gave Huck a treat (he'd missed his early morning walk) and headed out. The morning air was glacial, and a few clouds cluttered the sky. The island made it through the storm. Aside from fewer branches on trees and tiles on roofs, everything was back to normal. Frannie had posted her sign that let passengers know the ferry was temporarily out of service. I didn't see her onboard. She was probably taking the morning off. Aside from a few pelicans sitting on the railing waiting for the fishing boats to return, the wharf was deserted. It was too early for the kiosks and food stands to open. Their winter hours were short and sweet.

The hotel lobby was as deserted as the wharf. I spotted Jill wrapping silverware in napkins in the restaurant. I needed to talk to Arlene, but once again, I'd come during the wrong shift. I was sure Jill would tell me where I could find Arlene. I only hoped she'd be able to remember whether or not she saw Toni in the dining area.

"Morning, Jill," I said.

She looked up from her task. "Anna, how's it going? Are you here for breakfast?"

"No, not today."

Jill put down the set of silverware she was holding,

looked back over her shoulder, presumably to see if the manager was near, and walked closer to me. "Those two women, the ones whose friends were killed, were so mad this morning. They stepped out of the elevator with their luggage ready to take the ferry to the mainland, only the *Salty Bottom's* having engine trouble. They made quite a scene at the front desk, especially the tall one with the red hair. The other one, the one with the diamond watch and designer luggage, was on the phone. I assume she was trying to charter a boat or something."

I hadn't considered that Toni might try and hire a boat. "Did they leave?"

"I don't think so. I saw them pick up their bags and go back to the elevator."

"Thank goodness."

Jill moved even closer. "Is it true? Did that slouchy old detective arrest Samuel for the murders? Everyone knows Sam is the nicest guy in the world. There's no way he killed someone."

"I think we all know that, but unfortunately, that's how Norwich works. And now I need your help, Jill."

Her retainer clacked against her teeth as she smiled. "Sure thing. What do you need?"

"Can you tell me where I might find Arlene? I need to talk to her."

"Sure, I know where she's at. She picked up some early morning hours at Pirate's Gold. She's helping Jack with food prep. It's hard to make good money here in the offseason, so Arlene likes to take on a second job." My friend Jack Drake ran the Pirate's Gold restaurant on the boardwalk. It was a popular destination on the island due to our mostly fictional, pirate-y past. Even the island's museum displayed pirate relics, both fake and real, to fit in with our purported, but mostly made-up, history.

"Thanks so much, Jill."

Betsy and Toni were anxious to leave. That made sense. Carla would be stuck on the island as well, at least until the ferry started again. I could only assume she, too, tried to leave but discovered there was a delay and headed back to the cabin.

I hurried down the boardwalk to the restaurant. A big ship's wheel out front had a sign hanging on it that said there'd be fresh clam chowder today. In the summer, there'd be a waiting list to get in, but today, it would be mostly locals in for lunch. Revenue was slow for all the businesses in winter, but the summer months more than made up for it. Everyone knew it was feast or famine here. Famine was usually nice and quiet and a time to regroup, but not this weekend. This weekend had come in with a bang—a big, destructive storm. Even though the weather had passed, catastrophe was still in the air.

The restaurant was closed. I knocked several times on the door. Jack came out of the kitchen wearing an apron wrapped around his waist. He unlocked the door.

"Anna, what on earth is going on? I heard Sam got arrested for murder? I've been huddled at home all weekend." He stepped back.

"Come inside."

A heavy seafood odor wafted out from the steamy kitchen. "Is Arlene helping you this morning?"

"Yeah, she's in the kitchen. Why do you need Arlene?"

"I need to ask her a few questions. One of my suspects gave an alibi that she was in the hotel restaurant on Saturday afternoon at the same time that I—" I stopped. Jack didn't need to hear about my ordeal. I was ashamed of letting it happen. "I just need to ask her a few questions. I won't take up much of her time."

"Take all the time you need. I figured Sam's arrest was another one of Norwich's mistakes." Jack had, himself, faced a similar predicament when Norwich was ready to charge him for the murder of a man who'd opened a bakery next to his restaurant. Like now, I had to work fast to find the real culprit. I'd been able to stop Jack's arrest altogether. I hadn't been as fortunate with Samuel's predicament. The poor guy was on the mainland sitting in a jail cell for a crime he didn't commit.

Arlene was young, early twenties. She usually had her long brown hair pushed back behind a hairband. This morning it was tucked in a hairnet. She was wearing the same kind of apron as Jack, and her face was pearled with moisture from the steam over the stove.

"Arlene, Anna needs to ask you a few questions," Jack called.

Arlene's eyes rounded. She put the spoon she was holding down and wiped her hands on the apron. "Hi, Anna, I guess you're working on the case of those two dead women."

"*Two* dead women," Jack said on a gasp. "I've got to leave

my house more."

"I am working on that case. I don't know if you're aware, Arlene, but two other women, the surviving half of the four friends, are staying in the hotel."

Arlene nodded as I spoke. "I've seen both of them. One looks like she belongs on an Olympic ski team, and she's not very friendly. The other looks as if she lives in a mansion and has a butler, but she's nicer than the other one."

Jack and I exchanged impressed looks. "You have terrific attention to detail," I said. "Maybe I'll hand this job off to you when I'm tired of it."

Arlene laughed. "Only if there's a salary to go with it. I'm saving for a trip to Europe."

"No salary and unfortunately, except for intrinsic ones, no rewards either. Since you're so good at remembering things—"

Jack chuckled. "The joy of being in your twenties."

"Yes, indeed. Arlene, do you happen to remember seeing the rich woman eating in the dining room around three on Saturday afternoon?"

Her eyes rolled up to the side. "Let's see, Saturday afternoon. They were serving chicken picante for lunch and dinner. Wait, yes, she was there. But she didn't eat. She had a cup of coffee, then she was on the phone. She looked angry at the person on the other end."

"I know you'd never eavesdrop, but it might help the case. Did you happen to pick up anything in the conversation?"

"Not really. She was talking quietly but sort of frantically, if you know what I mean."

"How long did she stay?"

Arlene smiled. "That I remember because Sally was serving her table, and the woman left her a twenty-dollar tip. Sally was bragging that all she did was bring her one cup of coffee, and she got twenty bucks. She was only there for that cup of coffee, and the call was short. I'd say she was sitting there for twenty minutes total." That was all Toni needed to cover her alibi. Betsy knocked on her door and then, presumably, went back to her room. Toni didn't have to be gone long to miss seeing Betsy.

"Just one more thing—did you notice if she went back to her room after the coffee?"

"She went to the elevator, but I think she just went to her room to get her hat and gloves, because I was standing in the lobby replacing the lunch menu with the dinner menu, and I saw her step off the elevator all geared up to go out."

"Did you see her leave?"

"Yes."

"And do know when she came back?"

Arlene shook her head, disappointed. "Sorry, Anna, the dinner crowd started to come in, so I didn't notice her coming back."

"That's all right, Arlene, you've been a great help."

Jack walked me to the door. "Are you getting closer, Sherlock?" he asked.

"Gosh, I hope so."

"Me, too, and if you see Sera, tell her we're all thinking about Samuel. Hopefully, he'll be back on the island soon."

"Thanks, Jack, I'll let her know."

thirty-two

I LEFT the restaurant torn about who I should see next. Then fate stepped in and put Betsy in my direct path. She had been out for a walk, apparently. Her skin was pink from the cold, and she had her hair tied up in a ponytail. She was wearing running shoes and tight black leggings. And she didn't look that happy to see me, which was fine because I was also anxious to see her on her way. But Samuel had been unjustly accused, and two women had been murdered. Someone needed to pay for the crime.

"Betsy, hello, I was wondering if I could have a word."

She grunted like a grumpy teenager being told she couldn't go out for the night.

I plastered on my most pleasant, albeit fake, smile. "Yes, I feel the same way, too."

"I doubt it."

She was so obnoxious, I really wanted it to be her. The vision of her being led away in handcuffs would be the best possible ending to this tedious movie. "Ms. Archer? Correct?" I switched to a sterner tone because, frankly, I'd had it with her attitude.

"Yes."

"You and your friends came to this island and, for lack of a better phrase, turned it upside down."

"What are you still whining about?" she asked. "The detective already made an arrest. I can't believe we paid that much money to rent a house next to a serial killer."

"Samuel didn't kill your friends. Detective Norwich is well-known for being spectacularly wrong with his cases. I have the list of killers narrowed down to three people." We were standing in the middle of the boardwalk in broad daylight, so I felt confident that she wouldn't murder me where we stood.

Betsy's lip turned up in amusement. "That's right. You and that hot boyfriend of yours consider yourselves some kind of important investigators."

"All right, well, I'm not going to beat around the bush. When you were in high school, you had a full scholarship based on your athletic skills and then you blew it big time by getting caught smoking in the bathroom. An athlete who smokes? Really?" I added in an eye roll to let her know I liked her as much as she liked me. "Ariel was the one who got you in trouble. She ruined your college dreams."

Betsy's laugh was as unlikable as the rest of her. Then something seemed to occur to her, and she stopped laughing abruptly and scowled. "Toni has a big mouth. Why was she talking about me?"

"Toni didn't tell me that. It was Carla."

Some of the pink faded from her face. "She's still here? Where is she staying? I need to talk to that little creep." Her gloved fists balled up. Betsy looked like a woman who could defend herself or attack someone and cause damage. My mind shot back to my attack in the shed. Someone with a powerful arm hit me. Nate and I tried to figure out what was used by taking a closer look at the lump on my head. There were no distinguishing marks to help identify the weapon.

"We've had enough violence, don't you think?"

"What is it you want from me?" she asked. "Are you trying to say that I murdered Ariel because she told on me twenty years ago? She did me a favor. That college was my parents' dream, not mine. I didn't want to move out of town. I had a boyfriend and all my friends. I was glad when it happened."

There went my motive—if she was telling the truth. "So, there were no hard feelings after you lost the scholarship?"

"Sure, I was sore for a while and we didn't talk for a week or two, but that was mostly because I was grounded. My parents wouldn't let me see or talk to any friends. By the time my punishment was over, Ariel and I were back to hanging out together. I had no reason to kill her." She wasn't acting the least bit defensive, which led me to believe she was telling the truth.

"And losing out on your place on the cheer squad?" I asked.

She laughed again. "Seriously, who would hold a grudge about that? Honestly, I much preferred softball. It didn't come with the perks of getting to hang out with the football team but—" She shrugged. "I did all right when it came to boys."

Our chat had somehow lessened the tension between us. I'd never looked at Betsy as an ally, only an adversary. Maybe it was time to cross over that fence. "Since I have you here without Toni listening in—I discovered that she hangs out in a group that appears to study the Pillow Talk Killer."

Another laugh. This one less obnoxious. "Study is a nice word for their obsession. Toni was always a crime buff." She smirked at me. "I guess there are plenty of those around."

"To be clear—I was pushed into this role. As you see—we have no law enforcement on the island, and the local detective is as helpful as a boat with a hole." The conversation needed redirecting. "Back to Toni's crime group."

"Right. Well, they meet once a month to listen to crime podcasts and exchange things they've learned or discovered." She rolled her eyes at the last part. "But their main focus is on the PTK. They figure since the police aren't having any luck catching him that they'd do all the women in the area a favor and bring the monster to justice. So far, no luck."

"He is a particularly pernicious and clever serial killer."

"We thought that Rachel had been killed by the PTK. Even Toni was onboard with the theory, and she'd studied everything about those murders."

"Yes, only not everything is public knowledge. The two detectives working on the real case confirmed that Rachel was not killed by the PTK. And I assure you, the man Norwich arrested is innocent."

The breeze coming off the ocean was bitterly cold. We

both pulled our beanies lower. "If it wasn't him," Betsy said, "then it must've been Carla... or Toni," she said the last name with dread. "The killer has been next door, after all. Only she's in the next hotel suite."

"We don't know that yet. By the way, where is Toni?"

Betsy shrugged. "We were both planning on getting on the ferry, but it's not running yet. So much bad luck this weekend," she complained.

"Yes, especially for Rachel and Ariel," I reminded her.

Her face dropped. "You're right. My parents always told me I was too self-centered. I've been working on that, but it's not easy."

"Do you think Toni is in her room?"

"I'm not sure. We're both waiting for the ferry to start running. Do you think it'll take much longer?"

I couldn't possibly ask Frannie to delay another trip. "I think you'll be able to leave soon."

"Good, the sooner the better." Her eyes rounded. "I guess I won't be able to avoid Toni on the ferry. And what if Carla shows up, too? I'll be surrounded."

"You'll be on a ferry with other people and the captain. You'll be safe. In the meantime, if you see either woman, don't tell them I was asking questions about them. I'm not clear on any of this yet. No need to start rumors or upset people."

"Not a problem. I'm going to avoid conversations with everyone until I get off this darn island."

thirty-three

I NEEDED to go back up to the Graystone cabin. My conversation with Betsy had softened my belief that she was the killer. I hadn't checked her off the list entirely, but nothing about her seemed guilty. She was abrasive and not terribly likable, but there was no crime in that.

The hike up to the cabin would take me past Sera's tea shop. I needed to stop in and let her know I was on the job and not to worry, even though I was plenty worried. And that worry became more profound when I stepped into the tea shop and found Cora comforting Sera. Sera was crying as Cora stood with her arm around her shoulders. Fortunately, it was still early on a Monday, and there weren't any patrons at the tables.

"What's going on?" I asked.

Cora gently guided Sera to a stool to sit down. "I'll get you some tea."

I sat next to Sera. She blew her nose and gathered herself

with a few deep breaths. "Samuel called. He was waiting for his lawyer friend to get to the jail. The hair they found on the first victim was Sam's."

I groaned. "That's no surprise. But he has a reasonable explanation for how it got there. Norwich still has a flimsy case."

Sera's eyes were so puffy I barely recognized her. "Are you having any luck?"

"I'm on it. I'm just heading up to the Graystone cabin to talk to the woman who arrived here on her own. In a way, she was stalking the other women, and some of her statements don't add up."

"Well, you better hurry because Samuel said Norwich and his evidence team are on their way to the island do a top-to-bottom search of the Meyer property." Sera picked up the tea Cora placed in front of her. She took a bracing sip. "Thank you, Cora. I don't know what I'd do without you two."

"Frannie has taken her ferry out of commission for a few hours at my request," I said.

Sera was nodding. "I know. I texted her to see if she could slow down the harbor trips. Guess we both had the same idea. But Frannie said she'd received word that Norwich didn't want to wait, so he got his captain to hire a boat to carry his team across. They'll be here soon."

"I don't think they'll find much evidence." As I said it, something occurred to me. Both women seemed to notice the invisible lightbulb that went off over my head.

"What is it?" Cora asked. "Did you solve the murder?"

"Not yet, but the gears are turning." My phone beeped with a text.

It was Frannie. "I'm going to have to fire up this rusty tin can soon. I've got a few people waiting at the dock. No sign of any of your suspects yet."

"I understand. Stall as long as you can." Sera and Cora were both looking at me. "I've got to go. Seems like I'll be getting my exercise today."

"Where are you going?" Cora called as I headed out.

"First stop, the Meyer house." I pulled my phone out as I raced toward the beach house. I needed to call my unofficial partner, so I could bounce my new theory off him.

I got lucky and caught Nate at a time when he could answer his phone. "Hey, everything all right?"

I laughed. "It's sad that that's your first line of greeting every time I call you, but let me push past the humor. I was thinking about my attack. My decision to go to the house was random. No one would have known I was there. Also, why would the killer have returned to the shed?"

"Good question. Maybe they were looking for something that might incriminate them."

"Yes, possibly."

"Why are you breathing so hard?" His tone turned urgent. "Is someone chasing you?"

"Again, sad that you immediately jump to that alarming conclusion. I'm hurrying because Norwich will be here soon. He's coming with a team to look for more evidence to pin this on Samuel, and that brings me to my new theory. What if the killer showed up not to retrieve something incriminating but to place something incriminating at the crime scene? What if they were trying to frame someone? Someone like Samuel? They first tried to frame the PTK, but that didn't work. They needed to find another person to frame for the murders."

"Brilliant theory. Brilliant detective."

"Thanks. After you found me, we were both in a state of shock. We didn't stay long in the shed. If the killer planted evidence to frame Samuel, I need to find it before Norwich gets here."

"Seems like you're closing in on this. I wish I was with you. I've got to get back on the scaffolding. Be careful and keep me posted."

"I will."

I reached the Meyer house and circled around back to the shed. Instantly, a jolt of apprehension hit me. I looked around and shivered remembering the attack. I moved cautiously toward the shed. At least the bodies were gone. If evidence had been planted, a thorough search would have uncovered it, but fortunately for Samuel, Norwich never did a thorough job. But on this case, Norwich seemed determined to close the investigation with Samuel behind bars.

I pulled out my phone and turned on the flashlight. The tools were still piled in the corner of the shed and the table, now empty, took up most of the space inside. I moved slowly around the table, my feet crunching the grit on the ground. The paper flowers were now strewn around the floor. I turned toward the door at a sound, but there was nothing there. As badly as I wanted to leave the place, I had to be thorough. Samuel's future depended on it.

Nothing seemed out of place. I ran my light over the stack of folded beach chairs and spotted something black amidst the colorful fabric chairs. I pulled it free. It was Samuel's glove. I was right. My attacker came to further implicate Samuel in the murders. It started with Carla's false statement about hearing someone behind her when she was leaving the Meyer house. That was when the framing plan began, and the glove was the next step. He'd obviously dropped it in the house the morning he rushed in to help. The hair on the victim had been accidental, but it only helped further the diabolical plan... of the murderers. I'd been looking for one suspect, but what if there were two? I needed to see Olive.

thirty-four

OLIVE'S COTTAGE was on the opposite side of the island, but it was also on the way to the Graystone cabin at the top of Island Drive. It wouldn't be a usual visit with Olive, just one quick question.

Propelled by the adrenaline I was feeling that I'd solved the case, I jogged as fast as the icy trail would allow. It wouldn't help matters if I fell and broke an arm or ankle.

Olive's fireplace was churning out a nice cloud of smoke. I knocked. She opened the door. "Anna, I didn't expect to see you. Is everything all right? You look flushed. Come inside. I'll get you a glass of water."

"No time for that right now, Olive. I just need to ask you one quick question and then I'm off."

"Of course, what is it?"

"When Carla was here for her visit on Saturday, do you remember if she got a phone call?"

Olive rubbed her chin in thought, then her eyes brightened. "Yes, as a matter of fact she did. We were down in the basement painting, but she carried the phone upstairs to take the call."

"You didn't happen to pick up any of the conversation?" I asked.

"No. I can't hear much from the basement. It was a short call, and she looked a little flustered when she came back down. I asked her if everything was all right. She said it was just a customer complaint. Someone ordered a print from her, but it arrived with a crease. I know enough about customer complaints to know they can be upsetting."

"Do you happen to know what time the call came through?"

"Now that I *can* tell you easily because Johnny started asking for his three o'clock peanuts. He started up just before her call came through."

"That's what I thought. I'll see you soon, Olive, but for now, I've got a murder to solve."

"Oh, do be careful, Anna," Olive called as I headed back to the trail. I reached Island Drive and took a second to look at my phone. My theory had just gotten a nice push from Olive. Carla's alibi that she was at Olive's the afternoon I was attacked was solid. It meant she was not the person who hit me. I was sure the bump on my head was connected to the murders. Because of her visit with Olive, Carla had dropped to the bottom of the list. I hadn't considered that she might have had an accomplice.

I pulled up Carla's photography website. I scrolled through all the pictures. She had prints that were mostly out in nature. Along with her professional offerings, she posted a lot of anecdotes and blog posts about her life. That was where I found what I was looking for. If I'd scoured her site more closely before this, I might have saved Samuel the despair of being arrested. There were at least five photos of Carla and Toni together. Most were vacation photos. In one picture, they were sitting on a beach, and in another, they were dressed for a day on the slopes.

Toni had told me that she'd spoken to Carla a few times since high school, but she made it sound as if they were brief, meaningless interactions. That went along with what the group had told me—that none of them kept in contact with Carla. It seemed Toni was lying. It was an odd thing to lie about unless, of course, you were plotting a murder with that person. They were the two peripheral friends of the group. They were tolerated and got to be part of the gang, but the three main friends never really let them into their tight circle. I was sure Betsy had been next on their list.

I reached the north end of Island Drive. The tower of the lighthouse came into view. It was a beautiful day on the island, so it wasn't surprising when I spotted Carla out on the cliffs overlooking the lighthouse. She lifted her camera every few seconds to snap a photo. It seemed she wasn't in a hurry to leave the island yet. No rush now that the local detective had made an arrest. Toni and Carla were off the hook. Their plan had worked. They were fortunate enough to come to an island where law enforcement was scarce. Was that why they chose Frostfall as the location for the murders? I'd read more than one travel article describing our island as a charming, remote place to visit, but it always came with warnings that medical help and law enforcement were a ferry ride away. Maybe they'd been planning this for years, and they'd finally found the right destination to make it happen. The possibility of a storm that would throw the island into chaos and cut it off from civilization even more only sweetened the deal. Puzzle pieces were falling quickly and neatly into place.

The next idea that popped into my head was one Nate would frown upon. So far, everything I had was just a series of gathered facts and theories. Norwich would laugh in my face if I told him what I knew so far. It wasn't enough. I needed something concrete.

Carla was busy with her camera. She didn't notice me sneaking around the bend to the cabin. I walked up to the door and knocked just in case Toni was inside. Carla's luggage was still sitting in the same spot, waiting to be carried to the harbor for the ride to the mainland.

I turned the knob. It was unlocked. I glanced back down the road. No sign of Carla. The house had been cleaned up. I glanced around for something, anything that might be evidence. The place was spotless. My heart was beating so hard, I could almost hear it. The bedroom and bathroom were clean. She'd even emptied the bathroom trash.

I returned to the kitchen and opened each cabinet until I found the one holding the trash can. It was full. I took off my nice winter gloves, shoved them in my pocket and used a kitchen towel to push aside some bread crusts and empty yogurt containers. Detective work wasn't always glamorous or cool, like in the movies, but I'd always found that getting my hands dirty, or in this case, a dishtowel dirty, was the best way to find evidence. And once again, my persistence paid off. Halfway down, below the regular trash, I found a pale gray sweater and a pair of leather gloves. Both were smeared with blood. I pulled the items free.

"What are you doing in here?"

I spun around. Carla wore a menacing scowl, one that made me take a step back. But I didn't move far enough. I'd forgotten that the woman always carried a big stick. Her cane sliced through the air and struck me hard on the shoulder. It wasn't heavy like the object Toni had used to knock me out, but it still threw me off balance. I dropped the bloodied clothing and grabbed hold of the counter to keep from falling on the floor.

Carla didn't waste time. She moved with lightning speed considering her bad leg. She pushed the trash can over and lunged at me. I jutted my hands out and managed to push her off balance. This time her bad leg was working with me. She fell over to that side and smacked her shoulder painfully on the counter.

"It's too late. I've got evidence." I reached for the bloody clothes. As I leaned down, her fist came right up under my chin. My teeth clacked together, and my head snapped back. She grabbed the clothes and stumbled to the door. I caught the hood of her coat and swung her around. Without her cane it was easy to throw her off balance. She careened sideways and fell on the floor. This time keeping an eye on her fist, I leaned down and snatched the sweater from her grasp.

The gloves were a few feet away. I hurried to gather them up before she could push to her feet. I skirted around her, avoiding her hands as she grabbed at my ankles. I raced toward the door. I had no plan except to run. Her leg put her at a disadvantage.

I yanked open the door and came face-to-face with a pistol. Toni's diamond watch sparkled in the sunlight. Her grin was nothing short of evil. She held out her free hand while she kept the gun pointed directly at me. "I believe those belong to me."

My pulse was still racing from the physical struggle with Carla. I could feel it in my ears. These women had brutally and without conscience killed two women they knew well. I was sure they wouldn't think twice about killing a virtual stranger, especially one who knew with certainty what they'd done.

"Step back inside," Toni said. All the gentle kindness was gone. It seemed her obsession with crimes and serial killers was because she had the same tendencies. Perhaps it was more hero worship than interest in solving crimes.

I stepped back into the house.

"Sit on the couch," Toni ordered. "I need to figure out the quickest and cleanest way to get rid of you. We are conveniently close to the steep end of the island. I'm leaning toward a nice and neat cliffside fall. What do you think, Carla?"

Carla rubbed the hip she'd landed on. "I think that's a great idea."

thirty-five

THE GUN WAS POINTED DIRECTLY at me and only five feet away. I had no doubt Toni knew how to use it. I'd already seen her handiwork. Her demeanor had changed so drastically, Dr. Jekyll and Mr. Hyde came to mind. An awkward, chilling silence filled the Graystone cabin. Neither woman looked like the murdering type, but Nate had reminded me more than once that some of the worst wolves could often look like the most innocent of lambs.

This case had thrown me from the start. I'd blamed it on the chaos of the storm followed by my terrible bump on the head, but the real reason it had thrown me was because it was hard to believe either of these women had brutally murdered their high school friends. I was in no position to be the interrogator, but a conversation seemed my only choice to stall for time. I certainly didn't want to step off the sheer cliffs at the northern tip of the island. I also didn't want to get shot.

"So, whose idea was all this?" I gazed directly at Toni. She'd shot her friend in the back of the head. I was holding onto hope that she didn't have the courage to shoot someone face-to-face.

"It was Carla's," Toni said briskly.

Carla's face snapped her direction, and her mouth hung open in surprise. "That's not exactly true. You came up with the idea on that trip to Cabo. We were sitting on the beach, sipping iced teas, and you said we should destroy those women. They ruined our high school years."

Toni sighed. "Destroy does not mean murder."

"What else does it mean? Besides, what else was I supposed to think when you obsess over all those murder cases?" Carla looked at me for support. All I saw was a crack in their armor, and I was going to use it to my advantage. Something told me these two would turn tables on each other as fast as you could say *traitor*. That was the whole problem with both of them. Emotionally, they'd never left their high school years. How else could you hold onto a grudge for that long? Carla had more reason to hold onto it, but by all accounts, Toni had a posh, dream life. Why would she throw that away on a twenty-year grudge?

"I'm with Carla. If a friend told me they wanted to destroy someone, I'd think they were talking about murder," I said.

Carla lifted her chin. "See."

"Her opinion doesn't matter. She'll be dead soon, splattered on the rocks below. Then the ocean will carry her away and people will be asking, 'Gee, whatever happened to that meddlesome Anna who liked to pretend she was a detective?'" Toni waved the pistol. Every muscle in my body tensed until she relaxed her hand.

Carla laughed dryly. "Look who's talking! You were always telling me you were going to solve crimes. You were going to bring down the PTK, remember? Seems like you were pretending to be a detective, too." Carla was quickly becoming my favorite of the two.

"Just shut up, Carla. That's why the others couldn't stand you in high school. You were always an annoying little pest. Rachel used to call you exactly that. Whenever you were coming down the hall, she'd lean over and say 'Here comes that annoying little pest.'"

"Well, when they saw you, they called you—and I quote—'our free ride to the amusement park.' They only let you hang out with them because you paid for everything. It wasn't you they liked. It was your daddy's credit card."

I needed more than their bickering. It was confession time. "So, Carla, your footprints were outside the Meyer house. You were there, in the house. Toni let you in after everyone went to sleep."

Carla's cheek twitched. Her arm shot out, and she pointed at Toni. "She's the one who stabbed Rachel. I only wrote on the wall with lipstick. And she's the one who shot Ariel. She hit you on the head, too."

Toni's expression grew dark, and the barrel of the gun shifted Carla's direction. Carla's face turned white. "You wouldn't dare." Her voice was shaky. Considering Toni had already killed two people in cold blood, I think we both knew the answer. I certainly didn't want to be the cause of that.

"Carla, you are an accomplice, any way you look at it. Toni, I'm sure you can afford the best lawyer money can buy. More murders are only going to make it harder for that brilliant lawyer to get you off."

Toni sneered at me. "I won't need a lawyer because the real detective already has his killer, and the only two people who know the truth are going to be shark food very soon."

It took Carla a second to understand what she was implying. "Two? You don't mean me?"

"You're one of the two," Toni said. "You can't be trusted to keep our secret, so I'm going to have to send you off the cliff with her."

"That's how easily you would kill me?" Carla asked. Apparently, she'd forgotten how easily Toni killed Rachel and Ariel.

"I'm sorry to have to do it," Toni said in a tone that didn't convey one ounce of regret. "But I'm not going to jail."

Carla huffed. "Your family would make sure you went to one of those posh jails where they play tennis all morning and have expensive cotton sheets on the beds. I, on the other hand, will be in a dirty cell with some woman named Berta who killed, boiled and ate her neighbor because her sprinklers spotted Berta's car."

"See, I'm going to help you avoid that misery and Berta by killing you instead."

My phone beeped. Both women looked at me.

"That's probably Detective Norwich. I talked to him this morning and told him that I had proof you two were responsible for the deaths. He's on his way up here now." I was both amazed and slightly horrified at how easily I came up with that lie.

Carla gasped. "What have you done, Toni? I didn't want any of this. You made me do it." As quickly as she'd lunged at me, she lunged at Toni. The pistol went off, thankfully hitting only the wall. I jumped up and raced for the door.

"She's getting away, you idiot," Toni yelled.

I headed straight across Island Drive into the trees and shrubs at the base of Calico Peak. I paused to look back at the house. Toni ran out, still holding her gun. I had the advantage of knowing the island very well. I hurried around the base of the peak. Once my feet hit Calico Trail, I took off at a full run. Toni spotted me and was desperate enough to take a shot. It echoed across the island, sending birds from their winter perches and, no doubt, catching the attention of everyone on the island.

My feet were flying as I raced down the trail toward the harbor. I had to keep an eye out for icy spots and, at the same time, keep my ears open for footsteps behind me. It took me a few minutes to realize Toni was no longer pursuing me. Calico Trail would eventually take me along the river to the boarding house, and while locking myself safely at home was what I wanted to do, I had a job to finish. I veered off the trail to Island Drive and ended up at the harbor. Norwich and his team had arrived, and they were heading toward the Meyer house. He spotted me and laughed. "St. James? Out for a jog?"

It took a moment to catch my breath. "No, I've been out solving the murder."

He laughed again. "You're too late. I've already booked the killer. He's sitting in a jail cell right now."

"Samuel didn't have anything to do with it. His only mistake was helping us when the island was cut off from official help. Toni Margett and Carla Overton are up at the Graystone cabin. It was a high school grudge that motivated them. You know—motive? The thing you don't have for Samuel. They just confessed the whole thing to me. Toni shot at me as I ran from the cabin."

One of the evidence team looked at Norwich. "We did hear that shot, sir." I pitied the people who had to call Norwich "sir."

"I have the killer," someone called from up the road.

Toni was marching Carla down the road with a gun pointed at her. Carla limped badly and had a hard time walking without her cane. "She's confessed everything to me," Toni continued.

"She's lying," I said. "Toni committed both murders, but Carla was an accomplice. Toni killed the second victim with the gun she's holding."

Norwich grunted. He knew this was over, and it hadn't ended the way he hoped. He reached into his coat for his gun. "Drop the weapon, right now. Both of you on your knees!" The other officers pulled their guns as well.

Toni pretended to be shocked at first. She gave Norwich a "how dare you, do you know who my family is?" sort of look before she put the gun on the ground and begrudgingly dropped to her knees. Carla was sobbing, but Toni looked less contrite. She managed a mean glower my direction before they surrounded the women for arrest.

Frannie and Molly found me. "Thank goodness, you're all right," Molly said. "We heard a gunshot and..." She hugged me.

"You sure gave us a scare," Frannie said. "Uh oh, guess you gave someone else a scare too."

I looked back. Nate had just left the trail. His worried expression made my throat tighten. I didn't wait for him to reach me. I ran toward him and landed in one of the best hugs I've ever had.

thirty-six

SERA'S house was glowing with lights and happiness. She'd decided to throw a party for Samuel's homecoming. I held tightly to Nate's hand as we walked up the street to her house. I'd been holding him extra tight all week. It had been a trying one. The Meyer house had a sign in the front yard that read, "Keep Out—Police Crime Scene." With a little more persistence and a real evidence team, Norwich ended up with enough forensic evidence to charge both women with murder. Carla probably wouldn't do as much time as Toni, but then, Toni would, no doubt, bring in a top team of lawyers. It was hard to predict what either of their futures held, but for us here on Frostfall, we were back to normal.

"This was a good idea," I said. "Having a party for Samuel. He's such a great guy, and he went through a horrible ordeal."

"He's such a crack-up. He was telling me he was going to write a book about his days in prison. He said it with a straight face, as if he'd been locked up for years and not just thirty-six hours."

"Was it only thirty-six hours? It felt like weeks. I've never felt so much anxiety about solving a case. I knew I couldn't fail."

We reached the door and walked inside. "Surprise!" Sera's house was packed with people. Cora and Tobias were holding a sign that said "Thank you, Anna. We love you."

Samuel stepped out from the crowd with a shiny silver star badge in his hand. "This is for you. The woman who keeps us safe and keeps some of us out of jail," Sam said. He leaned over and kissed my cheek. "We're all here to honor you. Most especially me."

I looked at Nate. He was holding in a smile. "You knew about this," I said.

"I might have gotten a text or two about it."

Cora handed off her sign and came over to hug me. "I can tell you keeping this secret was killing me."

Sera laughed and handed me a glass of champagne. "She told me she might have to stay at the tea shop all week because she worried she might blurt it out."

"Well, I'm entirely surprised and utterly grateful." My gaze swept past all the smiling faces. I held up my glass. "To wonderful Frostfall Island. People call her a remote, quirky chunk of land, but she's *our* remote, quirky chunk of land."

"To Frostfall Island," everyone cheered.

Nate stepped forward. "And to Anna. People call her remote, quirky—" His lips rolled inward.

"Good thing you stopped before 'chunk,'" I said to a round of laughter.

"To our Anna," he said.

"To our Anna," everyone cheered.

Nate leaned closer and whispered in my ear. "To *my* Anna."

about the author

London Lovett is author of the Port Danby, Starfire, Firefly Junction, Scottie Ramone and Frostfall Island Cozy Mystery series. She loves getting caught up in a good mystery and baking delicious, new treats!

Learn more at:
www.londonlovett.com

Printed in Great Britain
by Amazon